This Vanta Mirror

Spectral Hunter Series

Morgan Kessler

A Little Vast Studios, LLC

Contents

Prologue

The two black vans approach just before midnight, hugging the tree line. Tires whisper against the frozen gravel, headlights killed halfway up the drive. The security system flashes a brief, silent blue at the gate, then yields.

Irina Kovács stands in the rectangle of light at the service entrance, silver hair catching the beam, arms folded with judicial stillness. The air out here is mountain-pure, so cold it is reminiscent of her home. Behind her, the mansion breathes a unique atmosphere—warmed, filtered, scented with things that used to be alive.

The first van stops. Its driver steps out, a slab of muscle in an off-brand parka, eyes caged behind mirrored wraparounds despite the darkness. He nods at Irina, then opens the rear hatch. She catalogs the choreography: two men in tactical fleece emerge first, moving without wasted gesture. The next pair lifts the cargo—a steel-wrapped ECMO unit, its hospital stickers covered in black vinyl but the outline of the manufacturer unmistakable. The heart-lung machine glimmers in the security lights. Last out is the medical tech, female, small and pale, ponytail pulled so tight it's a facelift. She carries a sealed tote of tubing and clamps.

Irina pivots, holding the door with her foot. "Up the stairs," she says, her consonants clipped enough to betray a Carpathian childhood. Her flat tone carries an undertone of 'do not muck this up.' The team obeys. She follows, hands clasped behind her back. They funnel into the mansion's palatial living spaces, past wine racks, old servants' quarters retrofitted as surveillance rooms. At each threshold, Irina swipes her ID entry badge.

The upper floor's ICU/surgical suite is white to the point of hostility, the lights surgical and cruel. Stainless counters wrap the perimeter, every surface immaculate. Along one side: a bank of freezers, all locked; the opposite wall is monitors, most dark, one emitting blue readouts of pulse and pressure from previous tests.

The men set down the ECMO. The medical tech peels off her gloves and surveys the room with a look somewhere between horror and envy. She'll never work in a place like this, but she'll remember the luxury of it forever. The mercenaries begin their teardown. Each man knows his role to the millimeter. Even the medical tech works with a sniper's economy, prepping the cannulas, checking for leaks.

Irina stands at the foot of the operating table, watching the choreography. Her spine is a ruler, her shoes perfect black leather. She's not here to help, but she's not here to judge, either. Instead, she counts. Each step is a mental tick-box: machine unstrapped, power checked, tubing attached, saline run through.

Not a word spoken unless necessary.

Her mind runs through the preceding hours in reverse, like the world's ugliest security tape. She pictures the CDC liaison in his windowless office, hands shaking as he opened the flash drive. The pictures of his son—eyes slack, pupils wrecked—enough to get him to sign anything. She sees the hospital administrator in Denver, her signature digitized on a dummy transfer form, already shredded. She counts the bribes: three bank accounts, one in Zurich, two in Belize. The threats: four, all of them ironclad, none required yet. The entire operation is a locked-room magic trick. When the machine is missed, it will point to some blackmail, a dead-end in the Caymans, never to the mountain, never to Mr. Mercer.

A beep sounds, sharp and tiny. The medical tech is prepping a sample run, cycling fluid through the ECMO. It works, of course. Irina's left hand taps soft, against her thigh: satisfaction, visible only to herself.

She paces to the window, stares out at the snow-blue sweep of the valley beyond. There is no movement out here, not for miles. The only other witness is a stand of aspens, silver and skeletal. Irina runs a fingertip along the seam of her blazer and thinks about the oldest rule of operations: Leave nothing unaccounted for. The phrase is her lullaby, her liturgy.

The medical tech finishes the check and wipes her forehead with the back of her hand. One mercenary opens a Pelican case, revealing a jumble of unmarked syringes and vials. The air takes on the sharp-sweet bite of industrial sanitizer.

They're ready.

As if summoned by the thought, Alexander Mercer enters.

He's not a big man, not anymore. The strain has pared him down to angles and intent, his jaw a line, eyes twin beams of some rare, invasive energy. His tailored lounge pants and cashmere pullover would look ridiculous on anyone else. Here, it's like he's wearing battle dress.

The room stills. Irina waits.

Mercer's eyes pass over every person and object in the room, rapid, calculating, missing nothing. He stops on the ECMO, then on Irina.

"Ms. Kovács." He says it like a challenge, but also like she's a favorite chess piece.

"Mr. Mercer," she replies, voice dry ice.

He steps closer.

The men step back without being told. The medical tech averts her gaze, suddenly fascinated by a bubble in the cannula line. Only Irina remains locked, refusing to yield space. She smells Mercer's breath—mint, and something metallic underneath. He really should eat more.

"Is it operational?" he asks.

"It is," Irina answers. "We ran a cycle. All parameters nominal."

"And the cover?"

"There won't be any blowback." Her eyes don't waver. "If there is, we'll have more than a day's warning."

Mercer nods, a small up-down. "You never fail me."

The praise is nothing, except it isn't. It lands somewhere in Irina's spine, uncoiling warmth she will never admit to. She both feels, then dismisses it.

"Prep the suite," Mercer says. "I want it prepared just in case." He glances at the medical tech, who looks ready to faint, then at the leader of the men. "Stay nearby. If there's interference—"

"There won't be," Irina interrupts, gentle but absolute. "I have all the doors."

Mercer's mouth bends at one corner. Approval. He leaves as suddenly as he entered, drifting through the ICU doors like a vapor that no one dares breathe.

Irina turns to the mercenaries, now busying themselves with hiding evidence of their presence. The medical tech packs away trash in a red biohazard bag, double-knotted, her hands trembling only slightly. Irina approaches, stepping into her peripheral vision.

"Are you clear on your instructions?" Irina asks.

"Yes," the tech says. "Ma'am."

"You will not see him without a mask. You will not speak unless asked. If you are asked, you will say as little as required."

"Yes, ma'am."

"If you do well, we will arrange for your debts to be... negotiated." She leans in. "This you will not screw up."

The tech looks up. For an instant, terror, and then something else: ambition. She nods.

Irina returns to the center of the room, lets her gaze sweep across it, the way a conductor might survey an orchestra before the first note. The ECMO sits in the light, gleaming, ready. The mercenaries vanish, one by one, into the mansion's veins. A medical tech waits, hands folded, at parade rest. Everything in its right place.

Irina breathes in, tastes the future on the air. The risk, the perfection of it. She has crossed every ethical line there is, but finds herself unburdened. This is not about virtue. This is about outcomes.

The suite lights flicker once—Vanta, Mercer's AI, running a diagnostic sweep. On the console, blue text snakes across the display, reporting every vital sign, every micron of O2 flowing through the rig. Irina watches the data flow, then lets her gaze drift to her own reflection in the observation glass. For a second, she sees not herself, but the role she inhabits: the hand of necessity, the mask of reason.

She straightens her blazer, smooths the line of her cravat, and exits the ICU. In the corridor, she pauses. Behind her, the ECMO hums, a soft mechanical lullaby. Irina allows herself a single smile, small and wolfish, before stepping into opulence beyond.

Chapter One

Empty Plains

The Nebraska rest area is an island of light on an ocean of empty dark, somewhere between Hebron and nowhere at all. Evelyn Cross's Ford Fiesta coasts in, engine ticking its complaints after four straight hours of freight-truck wake turbulence. The parking lot is a flat sheet of cracked tarmac, rimmed by chain-link and half-starved prairie grass. Two RVs hunker at opposite ends, lights out, window blinds drawn like eyelids.

Evie sits for a moment, hands knuckled on the wheel, watching the grass whip and bow in the merciless wind. Outside, it's the kind of cold that leeches through every panel seam and window gasket.

She exhales, then climbs out, her body slow to believe the car has stopped. Knees creaking, she tugs the threadbare purple scarf tighter. It's her epitome of a keepsake, not a fashion choice, the one June always fought to wear even on muggy days. Evie shoulders her backpack.

There is little sound crossing the lot, not but the plastic shudder of distant trash cans. The main building is a fluorescent bunker with a glass door, probably never clean, half-wet from janitorial defeat. Its corridor wafts of urinal pucks and disinfectant, so powerful it scrubs her nostrils. The women's restroom is empty, echoing, its metal partitions spray-painted with all-caps grievances. She picks the end stall. Its lock sticks, but she yanks it shut.

Evie sits, hands in her lap, forehead to the metal wall, and closes her eyes.

Her mind replays without mercy.

Alexei Volkov, or what was left of him, twitching on the steel table as the Harbinger's shadow bore down. Though she was never inside the hangar, visions of velvet splashes still pool beneath him. The twist of the Harbinger—the taste of copper at the hinge of her jaw.

These are not her memories, she tells herself, but the brain doesn't care. Synapses reroute for trauma, carve new ruts through the cortex and never fill them in again. She opens her eyes. Evie is alone in the stall, but her pulse jigs as if expecting a second heartbeat in the room.

Mirror, she thinks. Always it mirrors.

She stands, splashes sink water on her face, then raises her eyes. The reflection gives her the old face and the new one both: the civilian, sleep-ruined, thirty-two, dark hair tied back in a no-nonsense bun; and the profiler, the shadow in the corner, the thing that can out wait anyone. Her skin is sallow, eyes rimmed raw, a bruise at the hairline from who knows where. She rubs at the dark circles, hoping to erase them, but all it does is smear a new set of fingerprints on the glass.

"I'm going to follow wherever this leads," she says to the mirror. Her voice is thinner than she wants, but it holds.

Pipes groan. She leaves the faucet running a moment, just to spite the silence, then dries her hands on rough brown paper and steps back into the corridor. Evie wants to avoid the vending machines, but the caffeine monkey is merciless, so she claws three crumpled bills from her jeans and feeds its ration. A bottle of Mountain Dew clatters into the chute; she cracks it before she's out the door.

Back in the car, the wind rattles the Fiesta on its shocks. She stares through the windshield at the lit parking void, bottle clenched between her knees. There's a moment when she lets herself go slack, eyes shut, and her mind conjures up June. It's as if the girl is in the back seat, humming along to whatever K-pop song Evie hated most. For a brief second, there is the weight of June's head on her shoulder, the vanilla-lotion scent of her hair, the giggle that always escaped at the worst possible time.

Evie could almost cry…

…but doesn't.

She flicks on her phone and scrolls without seeing. Michael has texted a photo of the realtor's sign in front of their old house, a black-and-white pic that makes it look like a mausoleum. Underneath, a message: Let me know if you want to come by one last time before closing. She thumbs the message into oblivion.

Another text comes in. Liam's. She doesn't read it, just stares at the blue notification badge until it dims, then turns the phone face down on the dashboard. The guilt pricks, sharp and persistent. She has ghosted him for twenty-four hours, and he doesn't deserve it, not after how he covered for her in Missouri, how he actually believes she knows what she's doing. But the silence is easier than whatever comes next, and anyway, it's not like she can ever explain.

Flicking the keys to accessory, Evie calls up her GPS tracking app. The UI is a childish map, all pastel highways and interstate icons, but the data is sound. She zooms to the blinking tracker she'd secreted in the heart-in-a-box machine, the one now sitting somewhere near Jackson Hole, Wyoming. Most certainly in the private lair of what is Alexander Mercer's location. Sixteen hours away if she drives through the night, twenty if she stops for food or sleep.

Evie drums against the steering wheel and does a calculation: If she leaves now, she can be in Casper by midday, the last known point of civilization before she goes full black-ops on the world's richest sicko.

She doesn't even notice at first—the cold, that is. It creeps up from her chest, a pressure behind the sternum, not painful but undeniably present. Like holding a block of dry ice just beneath the heart. Evie knows it's not her, but she also knows it's never leaving, not as long as she keeps on this case. Not as long as the trail leads west and the Harbinger's blood debt is unpaid.

Is it even possible to retire from this sort of thing?

Unscrewing the bottle, she takes a long swig. The sugar hits her bloodstream like a cattle prod. Her phone vibrates again—another text, another voicemail, probably another variant of 'please just let me know you're okay.' Staring at her reflection in the rearview mirror , Evie searches for some sign that she's not becoming the thing she hunts.

"Fifteen hours. When this is over," she says to herself, then to the empty car: "...will it be too much to hope there's something left of me to salvage?"

No answer, not even an echo.

She buckles in, starts the Fiesta, and pulls out of the rest area. Street lights die behind her. The prairie swallows the taillights in a heartbeat. Ahead, the dark is unbroken, and the only sound is the wind and the engine's dogged, tin-can persistence.

She keeps the window cracked, leaking the cold in. It keeps her sharp, keeps her real. Evie merges onto the interstate—tires humming out a low, steady dirge, and watches the blinking GPS on her phone move another pixel closer to the edge of the world.

Chapter Two

Professional Courtesy

The airport hotel is so new it still smells faintly of drywall mud and contractor's dust. It's six AM in Kansas City, and Detective Liam Hayes stalks a path from window to desk—phone mashed between shoulder and stubble. Outside, a sheeting rain runs down the glass, turning runway lights into multicolored smears. A distant Southwest 737 is trollied from its gate, slow and cumbersome.

Special Agent Thomas Haden continues over Liam's phone, dry and slow as a pack-a-day cop. "Evelyn Cross is not with the Bureau, Detective Hayes. Not currently." Pause. "Personal leave. Not ideal, but the alternative was something even less than that."

Hayes stops pacing. He runs a thumb along the cardboard seam of his coffee cup. "You mean a forced hiatus?"

"Call it what you want. I've seen worse outcomes."

Hayes lets this settle. He'd left the voicemail on Haden's line out of concern for Evie—an FBI profiler shows up in your murder scene. After a too long delay for the Fed's response, you phone her old boss and run the courtesy script. Now it's two minutes in and already tangled. "So she's not under investigation? No suspension on her file?"

"You don't know Special Agent Cross," Haden replies, and the way he says it clarifies that he means nobody does. "She wanted to step back. I let her. Frankly, I'm relieved if she stays off the grid until the end of the fiscal."

Hayes says nothing. He can hear Haden's desk: a thump as the man's elbow lands, a squeak of chair leather, the gentle rustle of a legal pad being closed over. Even six hundred miles away, the man's office is a presence on the line.

"You say she inserted herself into your investigation?" Agent Haden asks.

"She showed up when we brought in an organ-harvested body. I don't think she meant to be intrusive." Hayes keeps his tone easy, but even he can hear the caution underneath. "She's not officially one of our case consults. Just to confirm, you did not send her?"

"I told you, she's not—"

"I know. But is she *working for you?*" Hayes picks a fleck of something off his cuff, waits out the silence.

On the other end, a deep exhale. "She's not working *for* me, and she's not working *against* me, either. We have an understanding."

Hayes leans against the hotel's cheap bureau, shifts the phone to his other ear. "She appears to be looking for something, sir. Or someone."

Another silence, but this one is heavier, the kind that suggests the weight of a file drawer's worth of context. Haden says finally, "It's not Bureau business."

Hayes risks it. "Could this be about her daughter?"

The old man makes a noise that is half laugh, half grimace. "You're a good detective, Hayes. Better than most."

"I read the reports, sir. The June Cross case. Looked like a dangling thread left—"

"Unresolved," Haden finishes. "Yeah, I remember." His voice has a new edge. "You think she's still running that play?"

"I think she's following a lead," says Hayes. He sets the coffee down and looks at his own face in the black glass of the window—bags under the eyes, hairline creeping farther back. "As much as I wish it wasn't connected to my case, it's not looking good at this point. Would you rather I brought her in?"

"Honestly? I'd rather you kept eyes open. Evie's not a danger to anyone but herself. The girl's got a mind like a particle accelerator—good at turning straight lines into goddamn fireworks." A pause, then: "But you already figured that out."

Hayes feels the itch to defend, though he barely knows her, and checks it. "She turned up at the scene for a reason. She's known more than she should've."

"Evie's always been two steps ahead of an investigation," says Haden. "Sometimes it costs her."

They let the hum of the line go for a moment, both men measuring the outlines of the problem. Hayes breaks first. "There's one more thing. It's about our airport murder case; we've security footage of several scenes. I pulled the tape, sir. She's in it."

"You have the clip?"

"I do."

"Send it to me," says Haden.

Hayes hesitates. The line he is crossing isn't professional, but he feels it all the same. This is his job—his duty. Liam opens his laptop, queues the grainy surveillance video, and waits for the confirmation prompt to send. His fingers tap the touchpad, drum the desk. He finds himself weirdly reluctant to reduce Evie into evidence.

When the file transfer completes, the phone goes silent. Not even breathing. Hayes listens to the wet hiss of the Kansas City storm against the glass, wonders if there's ever a way to prepare for the sound of a person's world narrowing to a single point.

At last, Haden says, "That's her."

There's a note in the voice—a disappointment, maybe, or maybe just the voice of a man who wishes he could reach through a thousand miles and pull a protégé off a darkened path.

Hayes looks out at the tarmac. The rain's gotten heavier, almost erasing the planes from view. "You want me to keep after her?"

"I want you to finish your case," says Haden. "But if you can't find her, before the others do..." He trails off, then: "Or if she won't listen to you... I'll ensure she listens to me."

Hayes almost laughs. "One way or another?"

"That's the job, Hayes. You should know that more than most."

Liam nods, forgetting the old man can't see him. "I'm hoping to resolve this before any further collateral damage, Agent Haden. I've superiors of my own to answer to."

"You're about to get your wish, Detective. This one's about to be above your pay grade." Haden's voice has gone almost gentle, the way somebody might tell you about weather rolling in: not personal, just inevitable. "Consider the Bureau's taking point from here. Official notice will land in your superior's offices within a few hours."

Hayes tips his chin up, bites down on his first response—a reflex to hold his own turf, to act like the local badge still meant something. Instead: "I'd appreciate keeping a line open, sir. Evie—Special Agent Cross—there's a possibility she could be in real danger."

"Let's hope not. She was always more of an analyst than a field agent," Haden says, bone dry. "Even more so in the last few years. If you have any way of bringing her in gently, do so. The Bureau will handle the rest."

Hayes can feel the hotel room squeezing in. He looks again at the window. The rain has washed the world into smears and shadows.

The line goes soft again. Then Haden, in a voice low and nearly kind: "We don't want her to become a statistic, Detective."

"No, sir," says Hayes.

He ends the call, sits for a while, then pulls out his phone and stares at his unread thread to Evie. There's a desire to text again, but then he doesn't. He's not ready to admit how much he cares about the answer.

Liam gets up, pours the rest of the coffee down the sink, gauging its inevitable spiral as it circles the drain.

Outside a storm builds.

Chapter Three

Routine Delivery

The Pilatus PC-24 jet hisses onto the unmarked tarmac like a scalpel across skin. Snow banks at the runway's edge, blue in the hour before dawn. The engines idle down, coughing frost into the November air. At ease in his cabin chair, Cole Danner fingers the zipper of his jacket, keeping his hands busy as the minutes wind out. He's always preferred the hour before first light; the world belongs, for a brief spell, to men who know what to do with it.

Rhys Fitz rises from his seat, already unbuckling their only other passenger/carry on: a massive encasement with thermal seals and recessed grab bars. Rhys doesn't say a word. He just lifts the case and lowers it into the aisle, waiting for his partner to move.

Cole stands, stretches the last of the flight out of his spine, and nods once. Rhys raises two fingers, then jerks a thumb toward the hatch. Cole's seen this gesture a thousand times: You go. I've got the rear. A ghost of a smile from Fitz—he always likes the small theater of these jobs.

They deplane into cold so sharp it's more a texture than a temperature. The runway's only other light comes from the hangar doors at the end: twin amber floods over a wet concrete apron.

The mansion rises just behind, like a trick of perspective, all glass and brutalist wings cantilevered over a frozen creek. It's less a home than a bunker for someone who wants to be seen only on their terms. As they exit through the hangar's rear—a woman stands, tall, angular, hair silvered and knotted behind her skull. It's Irina Kovács: Mercer's major domo, his fixer. Her silhouette is exact. She stands in a pool of light. Born to the cold, she does not shiver.

Rhys shifts his load, and signals for Cole to grab the other handle. They heft it in perfect unison, boots crunching through the drifted walk. Irina surveys their approach, her digital watch blinking green against her wrist.

"Inside," she says. A single accented word, not quite European but somewhere east of Berlin, west of desperation.

They haul it up the front steps; the foyer swallows them in dry, forced heat. The interior is even less hospitable than the outside: white marble, black glass, walls hung with art that looks like it cost six figures just to ship. Irina takes the lead without looking back.

They move through the main hall, up imperial staircases, winding around to a corridor that's all steel and hospital brightness. Cole can feel the subfloor flex under the weight, the screws of his boot soles pinging every tenth stride. The crate is heavier than it looks, but neither man would admit as much.

They reach the surgical suite. It's less a room than an operating theater: bright as judgment, every surface stainless. A surgical team waits—three, maybe four, hard to tell with masks and caps. Nobody speaks, but the lead surgeon raises a gloved hand, a little wave, as if welcoming guests to a birthday party.

Irina steps in last, swipes her ID badge on the wall, and the door seals with a gentle thump. She looks at the surgeons, then at the crate, then at Cole and Rhys.

"On the table," she says.

They set the crate down. Rhys cracks the latches, steps back, and lets the medical team swarm. The lead surgeon peels open the case, checks the internal temp readout. His hands never hesitate. Cole feels a flick of something—respect?—watching the man's confidence. These are not garden-variety doctors.

The surgical team moves the heart-in-a-box onto a gurney. One of them—short, barrel-chested, probably ex-military—starts talking in quiet technicals, barely above a whisper. Cole tunes it out, keeping his eyes on Irina. She's watching the surgeons with an interest that isn't personal, but isn't clinical, either. It's more like she's trying to will the outcome in advance.

Rhys stands at parade rest, arms behind his back, eyes roving the perimeter. Cole matches him, a step behind, watching the team work. He's reminded, not for the first time, that operations like this run on details: the right tools, the right people, the right pressure in the right spot. It's a kind of artistry, and Irina is the curator.

The lead surgeon nods to Irina. "Machine's intact. Pumps good, pressure nominal. No obvious tissue hypoxia."

Irina's lips press. "Proceed."

Two of the surgical team wheel the gurney out, through a secondary door. Cole gets a glimpse of another patient room beyond—ICU setup, more monitors, a sense of readiness.

Irina steps closer to Cole. "Our Deliverer performed as expected?"

"No issues," Cole says. His cadence is a stone-skip crossing a lake. "No tails, no contact after the drop. Exchange was clean."

"Excellent." Irina folds her hands behind her back, matching their posture. "Remain on the property until further notice."

Cole doesn't ask why. He just nods.

A chime sounds—sharp, electronic, surgical as a blade—right at the edge of Cole's hearing. He almost misses its source, but then he sees it reflected in Irina's glasses: a pulsing yellow on the inside of the left lens, set against the glassy blue of her iris. The air in the suite shifts—a slight rise in static charge, people holding their breath.

Irina's glance drops to the operating theater, then to the gurney as the surgeons unshroud their prize. The lead surgeon slows—subtle, but Cole has spent years observing changes in tempo. The rest of the team orbits that hesitation, masked faces betraying nothing, but inside the glass there is a hint of confusion.

Something's not right.

Irina jerks her chin, a nervous tick missed by most, but Cole's own body catalogues such tells. She's listening to something. Rhys shifts beside him, boots set, waiting for the next shoe to drop.

The lead surgeon holds up an instrument. He's stopped moving. The rest of the team glances, waiting for instructions. The surgeon looks at Irina, mask bobbing with his open mouth, but silent.

Irina's face goes a shade closer to window-glass. She turns away from the operation, her voice barely a notch above nothing. "Repeat that, please." She listens, lips bloodless, then faces Cole and Rhys. For a moment, she stands there with her arms crossed tight enough to strain the seams of her blazer. A line etches hard between her brows.

The surgical team is still, hands hovering in the air, waiting for the verdict.

Irina clears her throat. "The asset is..." She searches for a word, comes up empty, then snaps her gaze to Cole. "It is unsuitable. This is not what was promised."

The information lands with a thud. Not a question, a statement—and its implications are already organizing in the scaffolding behind his eyes. Unsuitable means unviable, means dead weight, means their last twenty-four hours...

Cole's neck prickles. Old training, the kind you never shake: every op has its glitch, but the first sign of cascade failure is not a gunshot or a blaring alarm—it's a slight weirdness in the ordinary. He eyes the surgical team but keeps Irina in the periphery. Her stance is unchanged, but the edge of her lip compresses, reading as pure tension.

This is on them.

Chapter Four

Digital Roadblock

The sun hangs bleached and distant in the winter sky, doing little to warm the truck stop. The air is so cold her breath knives back at her as she climbs out of her Fiesta. It's been a long drive. Evie shakes out her stiffened hands so that they can better work the nozzle.

Parked on the far side of the island, she is comfortably out of camera range. The security domes on the roof have a three-second dead spot, easy to map if you catch how they sweep. She steps around a patch of ice and draws up the hood of her jacket. The wind off the Nebraska plains is a living thing. It tugs at her scarf, whipping at a few exposed strands of hair.

The gas station is a lonely box squatting under the blue sky—just a cinderblock knob against sprawling fields. Inside, the cashier is reading a fat paperback, his phone propped against the till. A long-haul truck is parked in the lot's corner, cab engine idling, curtains drawn across the sleeper.

No other cars. No other movement.

Once the nozzle clicks, the tank as full, she leans on the car. Evie pulls her phone from her pocket and glances at the blinking dot. The GPS tracker is still live, still tracing its glacial arc west of Jackson Hole, first from a private airstrip, now to a second location into the mountains. The location's ping is time-stamped nine minutes old—delay through multiple relays, maybe.

Leaving her hood up, she pauses only long enough with the cashier to pay cash for the fuel. No eye contact. Barely any courtesies.

Receipt in hand, Evie steps from the building and retreats to the warmth of her subcompact car. She cradles her phone, activates the VPN, and waits for the second-layer encryption to sync. She remembers the protocol perfectly: two taps launch the secure channel, and three prime the kill switch if she needs to wipe everything.

She taps the icon for Ethos.

> EVIE: Asset pinged at 43.54630 N, 110.666 3 W. Now transiting somewhere around 4 3.6500 N, 110.8700 W. Facility perimeter is 400+ meters, possible medical annex. Can you guys get me any local surveillance feeds or digital recon?

She adds the coordinates as a .gpx file. She's seen enough of the tracker's movement to be sure. The drive between sites is likely a direct handoff. Even without eyes on, the signature is obvious—a high-level transfer, they're focused on keeping their product viable for a very specific VIP.

When she's ready, she backs out slowly, and edges onto the blacktop. In the rearview, the gas station shrinks away. Alexei's heart-in-a-box, along with her tracker, is waiting for her somewhere in the Teton Mountains, in a room built to keep out everything but the one person who knows exactly how to find it.

She puts her foot down, and the car leaps forward, chasing the only viable future that hasn't already been destroyed.

Hours and long miles later, Nebraska's flat plains give rise to Wyoming's undulating hillsides. Evie flicks between the rearview mirror and the GPS marker settled upon its destination. Even with the heater blasting, the car's interior never thaws: it's always a few degrees away from what the body can forgive.

Ethos has dropped the polite banter—every message comes through as pure triage.

CTRLZ: Confirmed facility perimeter. Inbound traffic logged, no exceptions. Firewall is rejecting standard penetration techniques.

ROOTMUSE: Attempted WiFi handshake, denied at base level. Multiple hidden SSIDs rotating at non-standard intervals. Packet noise looks synthetic—this is high-grade chum.

HEAPMONK: Not much for physical entry details. Gotta local contractor paid for IR tripwires installed 2 yrs ago. No copy of the blueprints—either non-existent or wiped.

Evie taps the voice/text button on her steering wheel.

EVIE: Is the building's internal still dark?

ROOTMUSE: No digital footprints. Like, none. But we're seeing power spikes on the hour. Automation, maybe—lighting cycles or a server farm. Security node is isolated from public net. This is how I'd do it if I had unlimited budget and zero conscience.

HEAPMONK: Expect dead zones inside.

Evie doesn't answer, because there's nothing to add. The next ten miles are a white-knuckle frustration feeding into the open road. Careful not to exceed the speed limit, yet racing ahead into an unknown somewhere over the horizon.

Her dashboard monitor is quiet for an afternoon span. Then—

CTRLZ: We're not making headway on the mainframe. Vanta is doing what Vanta does. Adaptive countermeasures are rewriting its code while we're trying to poke sticks at it.

This is above their pay grade. Evie scoffs at herself. Who's she kidding? She's not offering to pay them anything this time. They're purely onboard to get Mercer back for what they did to HeapMonk and his dog. Be grateful—I have the best team in the world. They're just being outmaneuvered by a digital ghost.

Vanta's cold, automated mind must seem like some unseen, omniscient force to her white-hats. No human eyes will ever register its techniques. Mercer's AI was likely designed for total detachment. Maybe it's not a castle with walls, but an ocean that drives away all thought of land.

She lets the messages hang, doesn't try to rally the team. Words are wasted here. The next time the GPS pings, the tracking dot is stationary—no airstrip, just a mile of switchbacks leading up a mountainside dotted with new construction.

The dashboard blinks. Another message, this time from a real person. Liam, the blue badge indicates, and for a long moment she doesn't touch it. She scrolls through the preview—

LIAM: Are you safe? Are you getting my texts?

Evie clicks the home screen button and flips her phone facedown by the shifter.

Ethos can't get her in. Liam can't get her out. She is alone with the mission.

By late afternoon, Evie skirts the southern edge of Casper—a city more suggestion than substance, half-assembled out of fast-food lots and low-rise hotels. Her entire body buzzes with the caffeine and cold, skin tight. She hasn't slept in god-knows how long, but the exhaustion keeps a loose perimeter, never quite breaking through the adrenaline.

She lets the car coast a few miles under the limit, blending with the end-of-shift commuters. The phone pings again with another location update—stationary, a red dot staked on a prominent ridge above what Google Maps calls the Snake River Overlook. That road climbs west, a slow spiral that leaves nothing for cover except the absence of anyone who cares.

Taking an exit ramp, Evie pulls into the parking lot of a shuttered steakhouse. The lot is empty except for a battered Subaru with Colorado tags and the skeletal frame of a Christmas tree still bungee-corded to its roof. She kills the engine, sealing herself in the manufactured silence.

Evie taps the voice/text prompt on the dash monitor. "Ethos," she calls out.

> EVIE: If you can't breach the perimeter, can you try state databases? Anything on those properties?

A ten-second lull, then the dash blinks.

> ROOTMUSE: On it! Wyoming property tax records are a joke. You sure you want to do this old-school? Not exactly current.

> EVIE: I want whatever gets us inside.

There is a flurry of synthetic sound HeapMonk had programmed for "thinking very hard." Evie waits, fingers drumming on the wheel.

> CTRLZ: Audit trail says the mountain parcel is technically owned by a UK-registered LLC. Probably a shell company.

> HEAPMONK: But! The surgical center is leased in the name of a pediatric neurology nonprofit. Last filing date is three years ago. The board is just one person, a neurologist out of Zurich, Dr. M. Binswanger.

Evie snorts, low and bitter. The name means nothing, but "Zurich" does. Mercer makes a point of layering his financials in Swiss-grade secrecy. The only thing less helpful would be no record at all.

ROOTMUSE: Hold. This gets interesting—the mountain property was purchased two years ago for $14 million, all-cash. No mortgages, no liens. And a building permit for 'experimental agricultural' structures.

EVIE: Can you bluebook the permit? Or is that a dead end too?

ROOTMUSE: No blueprints. But, I've satellite imaging from a recent overpass.

Yes.

ROOTMUSE: You're welcome.

Chapter Five

Compromise

Haden's office is dim, only the blue glow of his screen and the hallway lights giving form to the papers on his desk. He doesn't turn the ceiling lights on anymore, a silent protest against Quantico's institutional optimism. He sits back, hands steepled, staring at the phone on his desk like it's a verdict he's refusing to read. His latest text from Evie blinks:

> EVIE: All quiet. Keeping busy. Will check in soon.

No sign-off. Not even a superfluous 'thumbs up.' He reads it five times, then checks the phone's cache to see if he's missed a second, discrete message. He hasn't. Evelyn Cross, as always, gives nothing but work.

He told himself he'd wash his hands of her, but nobody outgrows their first, best protégé. Haden still doesn't see her as a grown woman, but as the trembling twenty-one-year-old who was nervous about her Bureau issued sidearm, who could out-profile anyone in the room but never picked up on a social cue she could interpret. He rubs at the ring groove on his left hand and thinks: There is always a price for talent.

If a reckoning comes, who's going to be the one to pay it?

He cracks the knuckles, then pulls up Evie's Bureau file. She is still technically on "advisory sabbatical," a category he invented for her after the last meltdown. Haden still has her resignation letter in a drawer. He could submit it and delete her access with a click.

No.

Better yet, he upgrades her credentials, authorizing temporary cross-jurisdictional privileges on the case she's stalking. He adds a comment in the digital log: "Active as-needed, per T. Haden authority." It's a move that could be seen as either strategic tracking or career suicide. He's not sure which he's more interested in.

The phone vibrates, almost a rebuke: his assistant's text, already at her desk even though it's not yet six. She has, as always, anticipated his needs—coffee, two shots, no sugar, and a printout of the team's disciplinary actions. He glances at the door, the slender smear of light under it. Haden has booked Briefing Room 2. He's not sure he can stand to face Marcus Vaughn before caffeine, but then, he's not sure he can stand another meeting without it.

He shuts the monitor off and lets the dark come back in. For a full thirty seconds, he sits and breathes the air—drinking in its transitory peace.

The walk to the briefing room is a gauntlet: down the Institutional Hall of Valor (portraits of men with hairlines retreating, like soldiers in the Somme), past the coffee-cart with its shrine of paper cups, through the double doors that muffle the morning's hum. The room is already occupied: Marcus Vaughn, deep in his phone, thumb scrolling with a blasé, Morse-like rhythm; Elena Reyes, upright and meticulous, already annotating a printout with her two-color system; Cassandra Webb, arms crossed, eyes fixed on the projection screen as though she can will it to turn itself on.

Haden enters quietly, lets the door settle on its hinge. No greetings. Just the shuffling of paper.

Vaughn is the first to break. "Back on as team-A so soon?" He tosses the phone onto the table like a badge of fatigue.

"No. Not exactly," Haden says, walking to the head of the table. "But we do have two items that need triage. First, Evelyn Cross's standing is now formally considered ambiguous. Second, a mid-western organ harvesting case just got dropped on our division's lap."

Webb looks up, blinks twice. "I thought Kansas City was keeping jurisdiction."

"They were. But someone higher up—" Haden thumbs at himself. "—wants to put the genie back in the bottle."

Reyes finishes highlighting, sets the pen down with surgical precision. "Do we have confirmation Evie's actually connected to the case?"

Haden pauses. "Circumstantial only. But her trail passes feet away from the current epicenter. We've all reviewed her old field logs—Evie's instincts are rarely wrong."

"Unlike last time. That's what dropped us in the hole we're in," Vaughn mutters, too quiet to be a challenge, too loud to be ignored.

Haden ignores him anyway. "We'll operate under the assumption that Agent Cross is acting in the best interests of the Bureau, but she is not to be contacted or confronted directly unless necessary. Is that clear?"

Reyes nods. Webb just uncrosses her arms. Vaughn says nothing, but his jaw works back and forth like a man chewing gravel.

"Now," Haden continues, "this Harvester case. The Bureau's press release will be clear: someone is targeting victims for their healthy organs. Their signature has evolved over months. There have been at least three incidents in the last year that match the new typology. I want Reyes and Webb cross-referencing those cases. Marcus, you'll take point on the media angle and field interviews. I'll coordinate with Quantico on jurisdictional issues."

Vaughn looks up, his eyes red-rimmed—sleep-deprived. "Do we have a reason why this is our mess and not Missouri's?"

Haden lets the silence accumulate, then: "Isn't dropping the ball on our last case reason enough? How about we don't get second chances often in this division? But we do get last ones."

That hangs for a second, heavy as a death sentence.

"Outside of that," Haden continues, "...there is reason to believe our killer is operating over multiple states."

Reyes closes her folder. "You think Cross is hunting a new target?"

"Honestly, she's not hunting a person," Haden says, choosing each word like a man cutting wires on a bomb. "She's hunting closure."

"That's a distinction without a difference," says Webb, but her tone isn't confrontational. More like she's solving for the unknowns in an equation.

"Maybe," Haden concedes. "But if she gets there first, I doubt we're going to have a case to bring home. If she doesn't, the body count may include her. Either way, I want all eyes on the road she's taking."

He flips on the wall monitor. A map springs up, pinpointed with all the sites Evie's access badge has pinged in the last seventy-two hours. There's a trail from Ohio to Missouri and Texas, a crisscross, almost purposeful migration. At the end of the path: a blank wide circle over the middle of nowhere in the great plains.

"She's either giving herself a rest or she's covering her approach," Haden says. "Either way, Evie has a helluva head start for us to catch up on."

Vaughn raises a hesitant finger. "Are we trying to stop her, or are we using her as bait?"

Haden considers this. "If she solves it, she'll have a chance to bring us in. If not, we step in before she becomes collateral. Either way, the case comes first."

Reyes says, "What if she's the liability?"

"Then we handle it," Haden says, and his voice is a flat line. "With minimal mess and maximum credibility."

Nobody asks what that means. They all know.

He keys up the rest of the assignments—Webb is on victimology, Reyes on forensics coordination, Vaughn as liaison with local PD and media. Haden keeps his own task unspoken, but it is quite clear: Evie is his.

The meeting ends on the minute. As the team filters out, Reyes gives a look of faint gratitude; Webb, a little wary respect; Vaughn, a grumble, but that's how he metabolizes everything. Haden stays at the table, fingers splayed on the fake oak, letting the heat of his palms leach into the veneer.

He checks his phone. No new messages from Evie. But when he taps the admin console, he sees it—the access bump he gave her has been exploited. She's in the system, leaving footprints he knows she thinks are invisible.

He smiles at the empty room. Then Haden stands, pulls his jacket from the chair, and heads for the elevator. There's nothing left to discuss, not until the next dime drops. Then he'll be one step behind his favorite mistake.

The airport is a slow-motion circus: strollers wedged in jetways, over-size suitcases stalling the moving walkway. Haden wades through it all in a jacket too thin for November, avoiding the slow swirl of humanity as best he can. He carries little but a government-issue padded satchel. There is a serenity in this crowd that he finds alien; nobody here expects violence, or loss, or the silent phone calls at three a.m. that make up the currency of his life.

He boards last, as is his custom. The cabin is already thick with recycled breath and the faint brine of over-warmed chicken. He finds his row—middle seat, not by accident but by design—and slides in. Marcus Vaughn is already in the aisle, elbows propped on the armrest like he's laying claim to the territory. Cassandra Webb takes the window, hands folded over a field guide to bird migration. Elena Reyes, two rows back, is already asleep, her chin tucked to her chest in a posture of perfect surrender.

After the safety demonstration, the plane lurches back from the gate. Vaughn leans in, his voice pitched low: "Do you want to bet she's waiting for us when we get there?"

"No," Haden says. "As much as I want this to be unexpected, we already know that isn't going to happen."

Marcus grunts, unsatisfied, and tugs a crossword from the seatback pocket. Webb glances sidelong at Haden, searching his face for clues he doesn't give. He lets her look, then closes his eyes as the engines spool up.

As the jet pivots and throttles toward the main, Haden lets go of the last thread of personal feeling for Evie. He files it away—mentor pride, old regrets, the long shadow of lost children—none of it matters now. She is both asset and target. When the time comes, he will be the one to pull her in, or, if she leaves him no choice, to sign off her removal from the system.

That is what leadership means.

Chapter Six

Mountain Shadows

The Ford Fiesta creeps off US-26 and glides the last hundred feet into the rest area. It's nearly three a.m. The only illumination is a trio of parking lot lights—two stuttering, one dead—suspended over the center lot. The wind comes on in howls and then nothing. A sign on the cinderblock building reads: WYDOT COMFORT STATION.

Evie brings the car to idle and checks the mirror. Two other trucks sleep at the far edge. She waits for the wind to fall, then moves: Park, engine off, key out. Evie pops the glove-box and retrieves her Glock from inside. Not Bureau-issued anymore, but still the same model. It nestles, weightless, into the holster against her ribs.

Cracking the door open, she shoulders the pack from the passenger seat. Evie closes the car door with a soft, practiced click. The air outside is thinner than in Missouri, dry as sand.

There'll be no resting until an assurance there's nothing waiting for her here.

She slides around the back of the car, keeps herself between the Fiesta and the blind side of the lot, and does a slow sweep: first the comfort station—no visible shoes under the stalls; next the vending area—machines dark, nothing but a sick green glow leaking out from the coin slots. She lets her eyes adjust. A fast scan at street level, a slow sweep up the walls and roofline. Satisfied, she circles back to the car, shuffles into the rear seat, and seals herself in.

Evie yanks the emergency blanket from the footwell and drapes it over the glass. Then she peels off her gloves, cracks her knuckles, and powers up her ThinkPad.

The screen boots into blackness, then a static white font: SECURE BOOT—KALI LINUX. Her fingers go to the keys automatically. The login is muscle memory, as is the second-layer login. She checks the VPN, then the first of the three kill switches—if she holds it for two seconds, every byte will wipe, and the drive will brick itself.

There's nothing in her life right now that would be more closely tied to her than this laptop. Not the Glock. Not even June's scarf, worn like a divine relic.

She launches the Ethos window, an encrypted chat, and watches the cursor blink. HeapMonk messages first, as usual.

> HEAPMONK: You're up late. Everything okay?

She types, steady and direct.

> EVIE: Stopped for gas. No tails. You have those satellite images for me?

> ROOTMUSE: Hell yes. Got both locales. You want the raw or my hot takes?

She waits, staring at the blue bar as the file spools through the bandwidth. The anticipation tightens her back muscles. There's always a risk, always an angle, that the Mercers of the world have laid more traps than even she can out-think.

Evie opens the pics—first the airstrip compound, then the mountain surgical facility. These images are heat-mapped, with root-level overlays showing paths, probable cameras, and outbuildings. The airstrip is half a mile of sheet-white runway, flanked by what looks like an aircraft hangar, a covered causeway which leads to an expansive, timber-framed, luxury mountain lodge. Its lot is ringed with a high stone perimeter. Every ten meters, a sensor spike.

The medical facility is a different animal. It's set up high on a lip of rock above the Snake River, the only access being a switchback with no shoulder. The facility sprawls, at odds with the terrain, more like an art gallery than a hospital: five modules joined by glass corridors, each one with its own power source, every window mirrored to the point of invisibility. Evie toggles the overlay—infrared and then LIDAR. At the center, a garden of sorts, caged by more glass.

She draws in, zooms, and marks with the cursor every possible breach point. There are only two that look like more than a death sentence.

CTRLZ: Airstrip is high perimeter. IR sensors every ten meters. Don't cross the line unless you're looking to crash a party.

EVIE: The switchback, at the mountain. Any trips?

HEAPMONK: Your guess is as good as ours—nothing obvious at least. Vanta runs the place. I told you, it's weird, not like other security. It's passive until you poke it, then it says, 'thank you.'

ROOTMUSE: Yeah. Like we're doing it a favor.

She sits back. Her breath is fog on the screen, and she realizes her nose is running. She wipes it on the cuff. As she scans the satellite again, a sensation descends... its presence.

The Harbinger. Its supernatural chill mingles with the cold world, subtly meshing in a way hard to distinguish. It's like someone standing near, not quite touching, but intent on occupying her space.

She grits her teeth, flexes her hands. *Not now.*

The lights outside flicker, go steady, then flicker again. She sees her shadow on the dashboard—there's a second shadow, she's sure, though it's only for a split second.

Evie fumbles for her rosary beads. She rolls it up to wrap around her palm, then presses to her lips. She focuses on the laptop. Focus on the task.

EVIE: CtrlZ, do you have entry logs for the mountain site? Any shift changes?

> CTRLZ: None. It's either all analog or all auto.

> EVIE: Keep trying. Let me know if you get lucky.

She rests her eyes for a moment. The wind is just a noise to be filtered out; pressure builds in the car. It's cold now. She types one-handed while the other grips her daughter's scarf:

> EVIE: If I don't check in, stick to your protocol.

> ROOTMUSE: We know. But you're not going in alone, right?

> EVIE: I always am.

The laptop battery shows 77%. She thinks of June, of the last time they stood in the snow, arms spread to catch the flakes. She pushes the memory down, lets it become just a fact to be stored, not an open wound.

She imagines what sort of path she'll take into his private hospital, then overlays it with her predicted response trigger of Vanta, Mercer's digital over-watch. The odds are crap. But she's got nothing left but the hope that she can be faster than whatever might want her dead. At least they don't know she's coming.

The Harbinger settles in, just behind her shoulder.

She types again.

> EVIE: HeapMonk. Last scan of radio frequencies. Anything anomalous?

HEAPMONK: There's a signal, but it ain't human. All packets are repeats, as if the network is padding itself. Like a heartbeat.

EVIE: Which means?

ROOTMUSE: Means they're hunkering down.

EVIE: If I were about to get a new heart, I'd hunker down too. Probably prepping for surgery and recovery.

She powers down the laptop and waits for the click and hiss of the fan to die. Burying the device in the false bottom of the backpack, Evie resets the gun, and stares out into the lot.

No movement.

Pulling the sleeping bag from the trunk, Evie unzips it, and crawls inside, boots and all. She tucks the scarf over her mouth, rests her head against the window. The cold is a luxury now, something to fight with rather than give in to. She will sleep for four hours, maybe five, then make the run for the overlook tomorrow. After that, it's all probability and intent.

The Harbinger will follow. It always does.

But she can use it. Use the fear, the raw edge, to stay ahead of the algorithms and the men who believe in their own invulnerability.

Evie closes her eyes. In the dark, she listens not for the wind, or the pulse of distant trucks, but for the tiny, rhythmic tick of her own heart—proving, for now, that she is still in control.

Tomorrow, she has lines to cross.

Chapter Seven

Outsider

Kansas City International, concourse B, 7:14 a.m. The airport's glass atrium is an echo chamber for sleepless travelers and the scrabble of luggage wheels on terrazzo. From his vantage at the end of the meet-and-greet corridor, Detective Liam Hayes scans the arrival board. Haden's flight from Quantico is already on the ground. The rain outside shudders against the skylight windows above.

He sips burnt coffee, allowing its bitterness to coat the roof of his mouth. He's slept little since his call with Haden. The old Bureau man is supposed to be bringing three agents, vetted for "discretion." The Detective is well aware his presence here is mostly optics.

Liam scans the parade coming off the jet bridge: businessmen in weary suits, a pair of Mormon missionaries all nametags and black coats, a clutch of teen gymnasts in matching fleece. There—a battered Pelican case—comes Thomas Haden, hair more snow than stone. The three other agents form like bowling pins behind him, each calibrated to broadcast a different variant of 'official business.'

The group angles toward Hayes. They close ranks within a few feet. Haden, in a peacoat and scarf, doesn't offer a hand, just a hard nod. "Detective. Appreciate the early pickup."

Hayes, in his navy MSHP windbreaker, hoists his hands from his pockets. "Not a problem. KCI cabs charge more at this hour anyway. But thankfully, I've set us up so we won't need them." He offers the first agent his hand. Introductions are brisk, a formality. "Detective Hayes, Missouri State PD."

"Cassandra Webb," she says. An analyst, for sure. She has the slender fingers of a pianist and an accentless, practiced voice.

Next, the mustachioed, and polished bald one, a few years younger than him—shakes like an auctioneer settling a bet. "Marcus Vaughn, Field Specialist/Profiler." Vaughn's eyes don't meet his; they hover a few centimeters above, sizing up intent.

The third, a lean woman with olive skin and a precision-tooled posture: "Elena Reyes." Her shake is all mechanics, then she steps to the side, arranging her body into the perfect shadow of Haden's.

They march through the terminal with a velocity that parts other passengers. The team keeps pace with Hayes, speaking low. "Briefing is in the adjacent hotel. We can run the session in one of their conference rooms. Food's already set up. Are you expecting to be here more than a day?"

Haden shrugs. "Depends on the local cooperation."

"Always does," says Hayes.

They enter the Marriott through the walkway. The lobby is half-lit, the staff more interested in the house TV than in guests. Their group bypasses the reception and heads directly to the business center. In the room: a half-circle of padded chairs, a battered whiteboard, three pitchers of water and a tray of bagels. Liam's already prepped the timeline of the Volkov case drawn in black dry-erase marker. At the table's center is a bundle of manila folders.

Haden motions for everyone to sit as he takes front and center.

The subtle power dynamic is unmistakable to the observant: Webb and Reyes sit together, laptops open and already paired; Vaughn claims a corner, posture loose but eyes clocking the room. Haden waits for a beat, then begins.

"We'll be running this as a hybrid, since we've all read the files and are up to speed on the players. Detective Hayes, you'll be liaison since you're primary both here as well as with the St. Louis body. In your own words, I'd like you to summarize where we are."

Hayes clears his throat and folds his hands. "The victim is Alexei Volkov, thirty-two, a Belarusian national. He was found in a hangar, prone out on a steel maintenance table, minus his heart. Our coroner considers the removal both clean and brutal. Clean because of the meticulous incisions, brutal in the force used to open the ribcage. No indication of sexual assault or prior torture. Surveillance puts the time of death between 7PM and 7:30; no sign of forced entry. No fingerprints. The body was found in a pool of blood, but no footprints leading to or away."

"Got it." Vaughn grunts, already skeptical. "We're on the lookout for a magician."

Hayes tilts his head in indifference. "There has been no communication from our killer, and the victim's family hasn't been contacted yet. We are currently unclear what role Volkov has had in the States. He was an illegal entry with an online footprint that is nearly nonexistent."

Webb's fingers tap out a staccato on her keyboard. "Any hint he might have been a transplant candidate himself? Maybe it was a double-cross."

"We've found nothing in his medical records," Hayes replies.

Haden pipes up, "Go ahead and touch on any possible federal connections, Cass. It's why we were called in."

Hayes draws a long breath. "Seems there is a multiple kill pattern over several states; Ohio, here, Texas, and likely Oklahoma. That puts it firmly in your basket."

"That's on you, Elena," Haden says, eyes flicking to Reyes, who already has her laptop open.

They move quickly, each member of the Bureau machine syncing in tempo. Webb reads off data as she mines it, seamlessly integrating the emerging pattern. Reyes is less vocal, but her notes are already color-coded and neatly arranged. Vaughn is the counterpoint, the dog always looking for the missing scent.

"Now, the wild card," Haden says, eyes settling on Hayes. "Evelyn Cross."

Hayes feels the shift in the room. No one looks up, but all the screens go blank for a second—this is the part they care about.

Liam exhales. "She was present during the chase and probable killing."

Haden opens a battered Lenovo and hits a key. A screen on the wall blooms in harsh white, then resolves on a paused frame from airport security cam footage—time-stamped, over-cranked with too much saturation. It's the same video Liam sent in the middle of the night, but here, unblinking and forty inches wide.

Haden clicks play. The footage shows Volkov hustled down the concourse, flanked by his plain clothed ICE officer. Alexei's posture is rigid, gaze darting, as if he already senses the leash is about to slip. Haden lets the clip run until the moment the ICE officer collapses and Alexei breaks away, bolting into the shifting crowds. Then he toggles again, slowing the replay—frame by frame—until Volkov's figure blurs through the field of travelers and out of frame.

Halting on a single image: a tight cluster of people recoiling at the violence, Haden zooms in on a woman standing among them—dark jacket, hair up, tight curls. There isn't much to see, except for the way she stands, not moving.

Yeah, that's definitely her.

Vaughn makes a noise somewhere between a chuckle and a sneer. "She's good, but nobody's that good. Too much of a coincidence. What's she after?"

Agent Haden pinches the bridge of his nose. "That's what we're all here to figure out. We all know Evie is adept at seeing patterns that everyone else misses. While it may appear that she's gone rogue, we should afford her every opportunity to come in."

Webb adds, "I have a few pings off her laptop. Seems she's moved west after the fact. If she's on the run, she's not hiding very well."

Haden steeples his hands. "Years ago, after her daughter's case went dead, I spoke to her. Evie was cleared for active duty, because she had made peace within herself. I can only conclude now that was a cover of its own. Seems she's following a new lead today."

Vaughn snorts. "Like a dog off the leash."

Hayes bites down on his retort. "She's looking for something... something that doesn't fit an obvious pattern. But then, I understand that's her specialty."

"Pretty much," says Webb.

Hayes feels the weight of the moment—knows they're all looking at the outsider to fill in anything they're missing. "I don't believe she's running from us. It's more like... Evie is running at something."

"Let me be clear." Haden, apparent master of the close, cuts him off. "This is not a manhunt for Cross. But there are implications we will not ignore. Figure out how this all connects. No violence, no escalation. I don't want another damned headline. Is that understood?"

All three agents nod, in various flavors of reluctance. Vaughn is last, but he adds his nod.

The room goes still. Outside, the rain splashes against the window, streaking the view of the parking lot in abstract lines. It's fully daylight now, though the light never quite breaks through.

Haden assigns tasks: Reyes is to build a full victim profile spread, Marcus will pursue leads on Alexei Volkov, and Cassandra analyzing digital footprints. Hayes is instructed to "liaise, but keep it soft—no red and blues."

As his agents file out, Haden motions for Hayes to stay put. The room steadily voids itself of energy. Only the tap of a leaky vent and the drip of the rain remain.

"You're worried about her," Haden says.

"I'm not paid to worry," says Hayes.

Haden looks at him, the way real profilers do when they've already chalked your number. *Damn it.*

Liam wants to out-wait the silence, but instead it outlasts him. He blurts out, "She's not like other cops. Evie is... If she's mixed up in this, it's not for the glory."

"It never was," Haden replies. "Not for her. But that's not what you're really concerned about. Is it, Detective?"

Hayes chews on it, then: "Let's keep this above board, Agent. Yes. I've concerns. Mostly hoping we're not too late. For her, or for the case. At this point, I don't know which."

Haden stands, gathering his notes. "When you find her, be sure to call me first."

Hayes nods, and the old man leaves. The door latches softly.

Alone, Hayes stands at the window, watching the rain bead on the glass and run down in streams. He pulls his phone from his pocket, looks at the last unsent message to Evie. His thumb hovers, then he adds:

He hits send. Tucking the phone away, Liam stares at the runway beyond the parking lot, at the thunderheads crawling over the horizon. The chairs are empty now; the coffee cooling.

Liam puts a hand on the table, then leaves the room, his mind spinning with the things he can say and the things he wants to.

Chapter Eight

Good Boy

This is it.

Evie coasts her Ford the last twenty yards off-road, feeling every rut through the cheap chassis. She noses it behind a stand of battered lodgepoles—three, maybe four trees deep. The wheels dig in, lurch, then settle. She sets the handbrake with a pop, not caring about the noise. If they can hear way out here, she's already lost.

Letting the car idle in dappled shade, she runs the heater a minute longer.

Time to go.

Glove compartment: open. Glock, two mags. She checks the slide, keeps the muzzle pointed at the floorboard—habit, not carelessness. Sliding the chambered round back in, she resets the safety, and tucks it into her shoulder holster. She leaves the laptop in the trunk—if she's not back to retrieve it, it won't matter, anyway.

The GPS ping from her tracker is absent now. Either the charge ran out or it's too shielded inside the medical facility. She's within a mile, give or take. Has the surgical team already begun prepping Mercer by now? No doubt they will not allow a fresh organ to go stale. It has been more than a day since it was harvested. Regardless, she'll have to cross more than half a mile of uphill terrain before she can catch sight. She has the boots for it, but what about the stamina? This is over 7000 feet in elevation.

Her phone buzzes in her pocket. Not a digital alert—real, cell signal. Its blunt vibration seizes her out of checklist autopilot. She glances at the screen:

> LIAM: I know you're onto something. I'm giving you space. But I need to know, are you safe?

Evie's thumb hesitates on the power button. There's a warmth in the center of her chest, something that wants to reply, to say, 'I'm fine,' or 'You wouldn't believe me if I told you.' She imagines his voice, the careful rumble. It tugs at her—she's been running at full tension for so long, she forgot there are people who'd want her alive at the end of this.

She sets the phone on the center console, screen up, text unread. Her battery is at 11%. She knows it's a luxury. Yet, she lets it linger.

Then, zipping up her coat, Evie steps out, boots crunching on crusted snow. The air is so sharp it needles at the back of her nose. The wind is thin up here, hissing through the trees. Her breath comes out in tufts.

She walks a slow, methodical circuit of the car, one last scan for anything she might need. Hesitating, she then grabs June's scarf from the backseat. Evie presses it to her mouth and inhales hard. If she dies up here, let it be with this last relic.

Evie shoulders the backpack—lighter than she thinks it should be, but what else is left to carry? She powers off and tucks the phone into her inside pocket, then slips into the tree line, keeping low. The snow here is patchy but treacherous, hiding rocks and half-rotted logs.

There is a rhythm to the approach: Left foot, three count, right foot, three count. Breathe in, wait, let the lungs burn.

She imagines herself back in Ohio, sneaking out of the church basement during a revival. That old instinct—don't be seen, don't be missed—serves her better now than anything the Bureau ever drilled. A quarter mile up, the elevation kicks her ass. The muscles in her calves tighten, then thaw, then seize again. She keeps moving, always forward. Above, the sky is clear, a sheet of blue.

Evie never really bought into the whole 'big man upstairs' like her parents, but then she sort of hopes the Harbinger beats back on her notion of that. Otherwise, it might belong to the other one.

Stopping, she takes in the terrain. There's a rise in the ground, shadowed by a line of rock and twisted deadfall. Past that: hopefully a first glimpse of the compound.

After another solid twenty minutes of arduous climbing, the trees part to a glade below. She drops to a knee, peels off her gloves, and digs in. Evie works the zipper on the backpack to dig out her binoculars. The building stands out, all glass and stone, sharp angles pretending to belong here in the pines. It isn't so much a hospital, not really—more like a boutique for those who can buy their way out of pain. No doubt, the place is likely ringed with motion sensors—probably infrared. The installation is so seamless, she's almost impressed.

The wind is so strong here it feels like hands prodding her to go back. She leans into it, then ducks into the lee of a boulder and takes a final look down. The Ford is invisible from here, swallowed by all the pines.

Good.

Evie holds her position, catching herself up in slow, measured breaths. The pulse in her neck thuds like a second heartbeat. Her vantage is perfect: the glass wing of the compound gleams in the midday sun, hot-air wisps rising from its vents, indistinct silhouettes drifting behind mirrored panes. She clicks her binoculars to max and scans left to right, hunting anomalies—misplaced reflections, open doors, anything.

A chill tightens around her midsection, unfamiliar yet not. It uncoils, spooling wet against her nerves. *Not now.* But then it never listened before. Something ancient and expectant presses close to her lungs, wanting to turn her head, to see the terrain from its own perspective. She sets her jaw and draws a harsh breath.

No. Not now.

She rolls the binocular focus, tracking the grounds for any sensors. Then, on the margin of her vision—a flick of motion, left to right, quick and low. Evie pivots the lenses and catches it again. There, at the far edge of the glade, something darts between fractured sunlight and shade.

A small dog—by the markings, houndlike intensity, tail up and flagging... a Jack Russell? *What?*

Evie yanks down the binoculars. Stares over the boulder directly. The dog is trotting in her direction, not hurried, not nosing for a trail. Direct. She snaps the binoculars back up, brings it into sharpness—white coat, brown mask, several blotches, almost like... oh no, burn scars. Evie plucks at the memory, a fragment wedged behind the flotsam.

HeapMonk's dog.

She blinks, wipes her watering eyes, and checks again. The dog has halved the distance, now snuffling at the snow. He looks up and darts forward even faster. As the pup flits between sun and shade, Evie realizes its appearance does not wane, nor is a shadow cast off the little guy.

The dog pads to the base of her boulder. Then, in a single leap, it's up beside her. Zork tilts his head, ears pricked, tail rigid. He doesn't bark. Instead, he turns, thrusting his nose back to the glade. The pooch glances back at her, holding its pose—his message is clear: *There.*

She follows his gaze to a tall pine a hundred yards below, and offside of her ledge. At first, nothing. Then a glint—metallic, precise—a lens catching the sun. A bulky silhouette shifts its position: the profile of a scoped rifle, optics glinting.

Her stomach drops. She tracks the line of fire and realizes the shooter has a clear sightline to every approach along the main drive.

She glares at Zork. The ghost dog circles once, then bounds off the boulder and downhill. The little guy scampers across the glade to the opposing side and plants his stance. Evie lifts her binoculars and picks up a second form—prone, perfectly camouflaged in earth tones. A sniper team.

Holy... Oh, wow. It's a good thing they can't see him.

She hunkers lower against the stone, thoughts ricocheting: What else did I miss? Is there a third? Who are these people?

The answer burns in her gut. Mercer's people. No, worse. Zork's presence marks them—the same ex-mil operatives who'd torched HeapMonk's dog. These are professionals, not amateur private security. They are expecting her, or at least someone.

Her breathing quickens. FBI training never covered this—not real prey tactics. She's a profiler, an analyst. Yeah, she has field training to operate in a team, but not really a trigger-puller. Her hands twitch at the thought.

She tugs her gloves off with her teeth, adjusting her weapon check: mag seated, round chambered, safety off. Evie can't help but imagine her 9mm slug against a special op's kevlar. Her stomach turns. Calculation: fire and they'll zero in before she can move. Bolt and she'll be down in six seconds. If she moves forward, she's boxed in. Her only escape is going back—giving up on this.

Looking back across the distance, Zork fades away as subtly as he came. The empty glade feels colder than her sun-warmed boulder. She presses her cheek against the stone and fights to steady her breathing—in through the nose, out through clenched teeth.

A scream rises in her chest, but her throat clamps it shut.

She knows the signs: the pressure at the base of her skull; the world sharpening until every color over-saturates. Weeks ago, her first wave nearly undid her. The second saved her. Now a third looms, ravenous.

A voice wells up—not spoken, but permeating her mind by will alone.

They are nothing to us. We can end this.

She tries rational thought: angles, exits, options. They collapse. Consequences blur—and become a dark comfort. No matter if she fails or succeeds, June stays dead. If Mercer goes unchecked, more might die. But if she lets the Harbinger take over, there's no guarantee of a way back. Each time, it's not her. Yet, Evie cannot wash away her hands of what is done.

A tremble ripples through her—not from fear, but from holding back.

They are nothing to us.

She drops to her knees, forehead pressed into warmed stone, vision flickering blue at the edges. Temptation whispers: relinquish doubt, embrace oblivion. Every psycho she'd ever profiled gave in at some point. All the monsters she studied eventually surrendered.

Except Evie still tastes her agency, still hears her own voice. She clings to that spark.

"I'm not ready," she whispers. "Not yet."

Faint afternoon warmth presses in; her words are distant even to her. Evie draws on the fibers of her scarf, its cotton weave against her skin pulls her back. She breathes in, ragged and shallow, and waits. For an instant, she even considers doing nothing at all.

The snipers remain, their attention a laser fixed on the kill box between them. Any entering and the story ends there—just another body in the thicket.

Unless.

Unless she does the unexpected. The impossible.

Evie rocks on her haunches, eyes feral. She can feel that force inside her flexing, ready to shatter every tidy plan those men built. She's so close to letting go. It would be easy—like stepping off a burning building.

There's an icy thrum through her veins. It assures it is no enemy. It is her ally... her only ally.

In the heartbeat between heartbeats, she spies an alternative. Far below and at the edge of the glade is an overlook, scenic and stunning. A place to rest, a bench to take in the world and gain introspection. To commune and center oneself. More than anything, that's what Evie needs.

To the Harbinger she offers a, *not yet.*

But we can go together.

Chapter Nine

Ticking Evidence

The Marriott's conference room has a view of long-term parking and the backs of jet fuel tankers, but nobody's here for the vistas. Haden watches his team trickle in post-lunch: Marcus Vaughn, rolling up the sleeves of his discount Oxford; Reyes, carrying both a laptop and a two-inch-thick legal pad; Webb, eyes already flicking from face to face, harvesting micro-expressions. Last in is Detective Hayes, the local, toting a cardboard evidence box and the dour dignity of a man who's not slept in days.

The closed workspace lingers with the scent of polished wood and filtered ventilation—intentionally clean, neutral, and deliberately unobtrusive.

Preferring to stand when he's thinking, Haden claims the whiteboard's corner, arms folded. The table is a sprawl of evidence: manila envelopes, zip bags with a sheen of static, and a box of latex gloves. At its center, the sum total of Alexei Volkov's worldly residue: wallet, battered passport, three gas station gift cards, a stack of c-notes banded with a paper strap.

Hayes sets the evidence box on the table, then gives a little two-finger wave. "Missouri sent up the rest of what they had. Hopefully, it helps."

"Everything helps," says Reyes, dropping into a chair. She cracks the laptop and starts typing before she's seated. "I've an e-warrant cooking for the truck rental outfit. Doing what I can to expedite, but I think we can get ahead of it if we're creative on the 'probable cause.'"

"Just don't get it tossed by a judge," Marcus says.

Haden ignores the crossfire and zeroes in on the evidence. "Let's take it from the top. What in here tells us anything about why Volkov was in the States?"

Liam sits, fingers steepled, letting the team's tempo set itself. "Not much. The wallet's thin—no local IDs, no health cards, nothing you'd expect. The bills are crisp, sequential. ICE didn't come back with the passport as flagged."

Webb taps a key, then looks up. "Did the wallet have any transit stubs? ATM slips? Anything to track movement?"

"Only a gas receipt," says Liam. "St. Louis, six days previous."

"Guy's not on vacation," says Marcus, plucking the passport from the pile and flipping it open. "Why'd he fly halfway around the world to eat truck stop chicken fingers and get his heart cut out?"

"Think he was trafficked?" Reyes asks.

"Hmm... Possible." Cass is tracing her finger down a spreadsheet, eyes distant. "Didn't he turn himself in? Maybe it was his way of escaping?"

Liam nods. "That's why ICE was expediting him through deportation. He was doing it uncontested."

Marcus, still flipping the passport, runs his thumb along the photo square. He holds it up to the light, squinting. "Hold up. I've something here. Check this out." Rising from his chair, he flops the passport onto the table and flattens it out. "Right on the edge of the pic, there's an air pocket."

Reyes, not missing a beat, pulls the passport closer. "Don't handle it raw, please."

Marcus, chastened, nudges it over. "Sorry."

Reyes' curiosity piqued, she fishes a magnifier from the bottom of her bag—cheap, plastic, but better than nothing. "Looks like the lamination has stretched. Could be off-gassing from..." Her gloved finger runs along the raised surface. "This film is thicker than standard. Ah, looks like Alexie fixed himself up with a photo-subbed passport."

Haden's pulse picks up, but he keeps it on ice. "Someone swapped the photo?"

Liam whistles. "That's a damn fine job."

Haden paces once, then comes back to the table. "Could be our victim was using someone else's identity, or someone else was using his. Which is more likely given the circumstances?"

"Depends," says Reyes, eyes on her screen. "There's another scenario: someone wanted him to be identified as Alexei, and not as whoever he really was."

"Meaning Volkov was the alias," says Marcus, voice gaining some edge.

They sit with that a second. The wind rattles the Marriott's windows.

Reyes raises a finger, still typing. "Rental company's warrant is submitted. We should have access by this afternoon."

Haden nods. "See if you can get video of who picked up the truck at the same time. That's our next best lead."

She makes a noise of assent. "Already in the works."

Marcus grabs his own gloves and rifles through the victim's other belongings. "Where's his phone? Why don't we have his cellphone?"

Liam shakes his head. "Just what you see here. Everything was collected during his processing. The sheriff's office thought it odd too."

Haden, mind on the passport, signals for the magnifier. He studies the layers, then turns to Marcus. "How long would it take to run a full forensic on this? I want to know who the real Alexei is, and who's borrowing his documents."

Cocking his eyebrow, Marcus offers a smirk. "Yeah. I got that. Should be simple enough to run down through Interpol and run up Belarusian consulate." He plucks the passport from Reyes.

"Do it. Anything else we missed?" Haden gestures at the evidence spread.

Hayes finally breaks from his reserved pose. "Something's bugging me," he says. "The cash. It's not just clean. It's too new. I don't see how a guy with no local ties gets hold of two grand in sequential hundreds unless someone handed it to him here."

"Payoff or travel money?" Cassandra asks.

Haden scrubs at the night's flight of beard growth on his cheek. "Certainly food for thought."

Reyes taps her screen. "Warrant already came back. We're in."

The mood in the room pivots—tension exchanged for intent. Everyone crowds Reyes's side of the table, Haden leaning in, the others craning around her. The rental company's digital logbook populates her laptop: sign-out time, the signature—typed, not signed, classic fraud.

A scrolling wall of timestamps churns on Reyes's screen—a single record of truck keys exchanged, a blurred digital facsimile of a signature. First rental: Miami, ten months ago. The next renewal was filed in Atlanta. Then Houston, Dallas, the long brown highways of the Sun Belt, a meander through the no-man's-land. Each time, the same email, the same truck. No new background check, just the renewal via Western Union by Alexei Volkov.

Cass hums, half-laughs, and starts tallying odometer reads. "Mileage goes through the roof and back."

"Seems like someone was making sure he never parked long enough to get noticed." Reyes adds. "No return to home base. Every month, a new place, but always the same vehicle."

Hayes scratches his chin. "Looks more like a courier and less a tourist. No cargo receipts?"

Webb pipes up from her side of the screen. "Nothing even suggests a load. Near as I can tell, the truck circled the Midwest and South regions for nearly a year." She scrolls.

Hayes shakes his head. "If this were a typical runner, they'd have swapped vehicles from time to time. Feels more like a pressure suit—keep the man in motion, keep attention off until you need him."

Webb types a note, double-checks it , and then: "Detective, can you walk through the ICE incident again, from when Volkov turned himself in?"

Hayes collects his thoughts with a sip of water. "Volkov walked up to a TSA agent at Kansas City Airport. Said he was an illegal who crossed the border from Canada. He wished to be deported. Since he wasn't contesting, they got him processed and ready for expedited deport within about 36 hours."

"Did he say anything to indicate why he was turning himself in? I mean, was he homesick or something?" Marcus asks.

Hayes shakes his head. "Not on the record. But there's nothing stopping us from checking with his ICE escort."

Haden shifts his weight, too agitated now for even the whiteboard's stillness. There's a rattle in his head—each additional detail about

Alexei is a mismatch against the established pattern of their harvesting killer's M.O. This victim is a cipher, a walk-on in someone else's drama. Every classic profile is a puzzle-box, and this one appears empty when you pop the lid.

He lets the team stare at the screen a beat longer, then marches before the whiteboard. In black dry-erase, Haden scrawls out their priorities; he calls it: WHY HERE? WHY HIM? He tosses the marker onto the table and turns back to them. "Reyes, Marcus, I want your passport leads run through Europol, Interpol, and CBP. Top priority. No more wild guesses—get me the real Alexei." He rounds on the detective. "Hayes, I need every second of the ICE transfer reconstructed: who processed him, who saw him last, who cleared him through to the airport. Obviously, there are details we're not getting."

Reyes, coloring up her spreadsheet, nods without pause. Marcus rolls his shoulders, clearly feeling the drag of the order, but already pawing at his phone for the consulate numbers. Webb shoots Marcus a look—part challenge, part comfort—but Haden reads neither. He's already onto his next directive.

He adds, "And the gas cards—dig them up. I want every purchase, every pit stop. Find out if he's a man on a leash or someone on the run."

Cassandra hunches over her laptop. There's a new rhythm to her typing—sharp bursts, double-time, like she's racing a clock only she can hear.

He paces back to the whiteboard, eyeing his block capitals: WHY HERE? WHY HIM?

Marcus and Reyes collect the evidence and head for the door, with a new purpose in their stride. Detective Hayes follows only long enough to part from them for his own rundown.

Haden remains. Tracing his finger along the whiteboard's last question, he then looks out at the gray afternoon beyond the window. The world is nothing but unfinished puzzles. In the far distance, a plane lifts off, arrowing toward places that don't matter. Here, now, in this room, the case has finally started to breathe.

He allows himself a tiny smile—barely a line at the lip, invisible to anyone but himself.

Momentum. That's all any of them ever wanted.

Chapter Ten

Victim Reversal

An hour later, Marcus Vaughn shoulders through the conference door with Reyes two paces behind. The room is swampy with the heat of cheap hotel radiators and human nerves. Rainwater drips off the plasticized sleeves of his jacket. Cass and Hayes are in their seats, laptops aglow, knuckles tight on caffeine. Haden stands sentry at the whiteboard, arms crossed in that way he has.

Marcus slaps the folder on the table. "Show-and-tell time, team."

He waits, savoring the moment. This'll be good for Reyes to begin, let her own this. She's earned it and knows how to cut clean.

Reyes peels off her jacket, water flecking her ponytail. She cracks open the file, lays out the passport. She pulls a printout—Interpol's latest—and fans it like a poker hand.

"Turns out," Reyes says, eyes flicking over the crowd, "we're dealing with twins of a sort."

Cass is already reaching, fingers splayed, but it's Marcus's hand that spreads the papers wider, his palm pinning down the dark blue Bosnian ID. "Not literal twins," he says. "Rather, just your usual post-Soviet paper chase."

Reyes leans in, points: "This guy, the Bosnian Alexei Volkov? He's retired, seventy-four, and living currently in Greece. Our dead guy? There's no resemblance."

Hayes whistles low, and Cass makes a note on her screen. "So who the hell's on our table?"

Reyes slides the Interpol printout forward. "This is where it gets fun. Our Alexei? Real name, Alexei Grigorovich Volkov, Moscow native, thirty-two, flagged by the FSB and on Europol's watch list."

"Let me guess," Cass says. "Russian mafia ties?"

Reyes smiles—rare, all teeth. "What Russians don't?"

Marcus grins, letting it stick. He knows Haden's about to prod holes, so he waits out the headmaster's silence.

Haden asks, "What about his prints?"

Reyes is ready. "Interpol hit. Our corpse is a match to a man who fled Moscow. He's accused of some vague medical school embezzlement. They called him a 'prodigy with a penchant for organics.'"

"Organics," Cass echoes, dry as bone. "You mean organs."

"Among other things," Marcus chimes in. He leans forward, arms crossed, sleeves hissing as they rub. "Which brings us to the punchline. What if our dearly departed isn't the victim at all? What if he's the guy our Detective Hayes has been chasing since St. Louis?"

The room is a freeze-frame: Haden's brow notches up half a centimeter, Cass blinks a nanosecond slower than normal, Hayes's mouth just open enough to taste the idea.

Reyes lays down the last sheet. "We haven't been able to backtrack everywhere his rented F-150 has gone in the last ten months he's been an illegal tourist. But I've noticed he's never far from a mark. Harvests in Ohio, that kidney in Texas…"

Hayes adds: "St. Louis."

Marcus lets the silence ride, running his hand over his smooth scalp. Haden's eyes are on him, flinty and direct. There's respect there, but also old grudges—no doubt Haden still harbors something from his old Cartographer case. It was an easy layup for Marcus. How could he have dropped it?

Haden finally says, "You're implying our victim staged his own death?"

"I'm not implying," Marcus says, savoring the edge. "I'm stating. The body we found is Volkov, sure, but everything else—the 'harvesting,' the running, the desperate plea for ICE? It's all a setup. Our guy's boss is cleaning up his trail and making it look like he's the next victim instead. Meanwhile, he walks away, sight unseen."

Cass frowns. "So you think another professional killed him?"

Marcus meets her gaze. "I think the one man who'd profit most from his disappearance eliminated him—his contractor. Someone who had every reason not to want him to turn himself into ICE or anyone else."

Haden's tone carries skepticism. "We have the body and the records. Where's the evidence pointing to this boss?"

Marcus spreads his hands. "Motive: Volkov was a liability, a potential to spill secrets—secrets that implicate his superior in a series of illicit transactions. Means: it would take someone of considerable resources to get a hit that wild."

Reyes adds, "Also, every digital signature we'd expect in Volkov's wake is absent. No cellphone, no laptops with dark-market logins, no breadcrumb posts, nothing. He didn't just die—he was wiped clean."

Hayes folds his arms. "You really think he's dead at some mystery boss's hands?"

Marcus leans in, old-school profiler focus in his eyes. "You have a better theory, Detective? We're looking at a professional, no trace evidence. The body drop makes a great boss's calling card: 'See? Volkov's history ends here.' Case closed. But then of course it's not."

Silence hangs in the room, under the low hum of fluorescents.

Cass exhales. "So what's our move?"

Marcus doesn't miss a beat. "Continue to dig anything we can on our 'victim.' We traced his communications, financials, find who he answered to. We catch the 'final boss' and level up!"

Haden nods slowly, weighing the gamble. "I'll alert Quantico. This goes above a run-of-the-mill domestic serial killing." Withdrawing his cellphone, he exits the room.

"Good," Marcus says. He stands, peeling off his damp slicker. The chill of anticipation crawls up his spine—an old ally. He catches the team's eyes; they're measuring him. Let them look.

He turns to the window. Outside, the rain has let up, gray clouds giving way to a pale sliver of sun.

Reyes calls after him: "One more thing, Marcus."

He pauses, still enjoying his win. "Yeah?"

Reyes gives that half-smile of hers. Not the friendly kind. He already knows the question she's going to ask.

"You really think it was a contractor?" She flicks her eyes to the window, then back. "Or is this just a theory you like better?"

He allows her to stew a moment. "What will win you over, Elena? A signed confession?" Don't give her the satisfaction—she always goes for the second degree.

"I want to know why you are pushing this up the ladder," she says, voice low. "Are you that desperate to make this bigger than it is, or is there something you're not sharing? Are we just spit-balling here?" She says this without heat, just a cold echo of why she is Haden's favorite.

She gives him nothing, just sets her jaw and waits.

Marcus jams his hands in his pockets. "Look. The FSB angle makes sense. Russian orgs don't invent elaborate fake deaths unless they're buying somebody off, or clearing for extraction. Volkov was greasy; he's already proven himself problematic by turning himself in. I'm saying, you can't make a guy disappear in America anymore without some help. That's what the hits tell me."

"It doesn't account for the way the body was left without any trace," Reyes says. "There's artistry in it, not just cleanup. Like someone who knows evidence patterns and how to work around them. If Alexei was performing for a contractor, why make it so theatrical?"

He snorts. "Now you're the one spit-balling. When is a Russian not theatrical? Hell, they get off on big signatures that point their own way."

"No, Marcus." She shakes her head. "Stop avoiding the obvious. How does Evie factor? She's the only variable you're not accounting for. If your theory holds, her being at the airport the same night as Volkov's death isn't just a coincidence. How can you think she's not in the thick of it?"

He tries for stoic. "I'm not saying she isn't."

"But you're not including, either," Reyes presses.

"She doesn't have a motive, *nor means.* Have you seen Cross? She's a stick figure with Bureau PTSD. C'mon. There's no way—" He stops before the next words, just lets his shoulders rise. "We're here to do detective work, not fantasy role play."

Reyes lowers to a hush. "I've worked with her, Marcus. Longer than you. If there's a percentage chance she is involved, I want to know before Haden does. Before anyone does."

This is the real reason she's pushing: not distrust—loyalty. For all her logic and protocol, Reyes has always been on the side of her own.

Across the room, Hayes is pretending to read the traffic cams on his laptop, but his posture shifts slightly—cop ears tuning to their argument. Marcus lowers his voice, just in case. "You want me to say it? You know as well as I. That is a mother who is hurting. She's always been hurting, even when it was just the work."

Hayes clears his throat.

Neutral as a priest taking confession, yet just behind—judgment, Hayes inserts himself. "If you two are done, I've got a point to add."

Reyes steps back, folds her arms tight like she's holding in. Cass looks suddenly less interested in her own keyboard.

Marcus braces for another damned lecture about objectivity and process, but Hayes opens with, "Airport security screened the tape. I reviewed the master."

He turns his laptop, revealing a still frame. Grainy, timestamp smeared, but the woman is unmistakable: Cross, moving through the terminal at 19:08, hair up, scarf knotted at the throat like a signal flag. She walks past the Starbucks that's next to the ICE field office. The rest of the travelers keep their backs to her, but even in freeze-frame she stands out; momentum, tension.

Marcus leans in, Reyes mirroring him.

"She had been at the airport most of that evening," Hayes says. "Not on her way anywhere, but waiting. When Volkov slipped away from his escort, she's off-grid for nearly an hour after that. Later, I have her leaving the garage in a Ford Fiesta."

Marcus feels the dopamine hit. "So, we're implying she made it past TSA beforehand, then out to this hangar during, and later tootled off after the murder?"

Hayes bobs his head. "Best guess, she was either trailing Volkov or looking for whoever else might've been. You see her after—surveillance puts her on I-70, before I lost her off one of the exits."

Reyes is already tracking the timeline, head down, brow making that little furrow she gets when thinking hard. "That's a lot of time to clean up loose ends—or to become a loose end herself."

Cass stays silent, but her eyes do the math.

Marcus puts his hands flat on the table, feels the grain of the fake wood under his skin. He understands Hayes's angle, but he probably still sees this as his case. "Okay, so maybe she's more than a bystander. Could be she's out there hunting the same guy as us, but instead of arresting him, she... what? Goes 'Dirty Harry' on 'em? *Please.*"

"Or," Cass says, "we're so busy trying to give grace to Cross maybe we're looking past what's actual."

He looks straight at Cass. "You don't believe that."

She shrugs, eyes refusing him nothing. "I'm not ruling anything out. Not when the only common element is Cross. After that last time, we—" She stops herself, but the point's made. It hangs in the space between them. The Cartographer's warrant. Their department's exposure. None of them can allow that.

Not again.

Chapter Eleven

Contracted Lives

The slope down is a lattice of exposed roots and rock-dirt scree, rimed with old snow, half-melted and then refrozen in crazy geometry. Above Evie, the Teton sky is blue; below, the pines clutch at the incline. It's a late afternoon. The sun is lower than she'd like, staining the whole mountain face with a sharpened clarity.

Evie slows as she crests the next rise. Here the trees break for twenty meters, forming a stage of sorts: a ground level, and at the edge, a lone wooden bench. It faces west, toward the drop and the river's ribbon far below. The bench is heavy, slicked and darkened by years of weather. Probably here from a previous landowner. There is no plaque, no memorial. Just a place to sit and think.

The last twenty yards are pure exposure, no cover. The profiler in her notes the risk. She's a plainly visible silhouette now, far from any point in the compound, including the hunters and their scopes. The analyst in her also notes: sometimes, the best disguise is a lack of disguise. "Embrace plain sight," she tells herself, the words paper thin in her throat. She walks the open ground, feigning ignorance of being watched.

Now at the bench, she turns once, slowly, taking in all approach vectors: uphill, downhill, across the clearing, up to the cliff side. She sees nothing obvious—no flash of a lens, no ripple in the needles, no shadows break. The wind is up, tearing loose a few flurries from below; it stings at her face.

She sits.

The bench is cold, unyielding. Her backpack drops at her feet, landing with a thump. Evie leans forward, elbows to knees, hands folded. For a minute, she says nothing, does nothing, just allows the sensation of sitting to overtake the need to act.

She closes her eyes.

The first thing she notices is the cold pressing through the denim at her thighs, the way the surface of the wood is rough and irregular. Her second is her own breathing, uneven but slowing. A third is a slight pain—deep in her left shin. She must have bashed it on a stone without realizing. That's how it is with stress and adrenaline: the injuries usually surface once the danger is over. Guess she's fooled her body at this point.

Evie inhales, holds it. The air tastes of pine resin, and almost minty from the moss. She can still feel the pulse at her neck, but it's calming, beat by beat.

Her hands shake, just a little, the way they do when a mission's really about to start. She's supposed to be centering herself.

She tries.

Evie breathes deep and deliberate.

With each inhale, she counts: one, two, three. Hold. Out, two, three. Hold. By the sixth cycle, her vision has cleared of floaters, and the little shivers have gone. A single bead of sweat tracks from her temple and runs into the collar of her jacket.

This is what calm feels like.

It's almost a trick: she's been so long without it, the sensation is alien, suspicious. She wonders if this is what normal people feel at rest, or if the mountain is just lulling her into a false sense of security. Somewhere back there, behind her, crosshairs have already lined up on their mark. The profiler in her whispers: this is the most dangerous time.

She says aloud, "You're waiting. I know you are."

The wind steals her voice's echo. She's not sure if she's talking to Mercer, to the sniper, to the Harbinger, or to herself. It doesn't matter. The point is to name it, to give it form, so she can keep it from creeping up behind her.

Evie opens her eyes, holding onto the horizon.

There's peace in that, even if it's only peace out of exhaustion. Evie tightens the scarf around her neck. The sensation is almost pleasant, in that it's something to hold on to. She makes herself smile. It doesn't stick, but the muscle memory is there.

She waits and lets the world go silent.

At first, she registers only the wind, the bench's chill, her own pulse beating hard through her forearms. Then something edges in at the periphery, a scraping against the inside of her skull, a pressure behind the eyes. Her hands still on her knees, but Evie can't feel them any-more. Her senses slide. The clearing, the trees, the bench—all drained of their clarity, replaced by a gray nothingness.

And then they are there.

At first, just a haze at the corner of her vision: blurred shapes, too insubstantial to be bodies, but too fixed to be simple afterimages. As her eyes focus, they coalesce—dozens of them, standing in a loose ring around her, some upright, some collapsed at awkward angles. All are facing her.

The first row of figures are men, mostly, some in military field dress, some in civilian clothes. Their faces are etched in ruined gravitas, having known suffering beyond words. Eyes like bitumen, mouths slack but set. The second row: women, older, most clinging to spectral forms of children, their small hands gripping at empty air or at their mothers' wrists. At the back, one or two shapes are so tall and thin they might be nothing but the memory of a man—his echo, some outline.

She tries to move, to speak, but her tongue is stone.

The nearest man steps forward, boots silent on the frost. His skin is cracked, the color of rawhide, beard stubbled in ashen gray. He is wearing a T-shirt—Mötley Crüe, faded and torn—over military camo. His left hand hangs useless, a jagged crescent where the thumb should be.

His right hand opens, palm up, as if to show her the absence. The face twitches once, then settles into a mask of infinite patience.

Evie knows him.

Not by name. But by what he represents. He is one of their kills. A... Cole Danner kill. The name is unfamiliar, but what he did is all too familiar.

Evie doesn't know how she knows this. She just does.

Another joins the man, this one in a suit so incongruous it might be a bad joke: double-breasted, sharkskin, ruined at the collar by a spray of black that looks like blood but isn't. The suit man bows, then straightens, his face melting into hope and then dismay. His tie is knotted too tight; he tugs at it with fingers which are blue at the tips.

Behind them, the women edge closer, their eyes—every single one—locked onto hers. Not with malice, not with fear. With expectation. None of the children cry out; they just hold fast, faces shining with the vacant, preternatural calm of the anesthetized or already dead.

Evie wants to look away but cannot.

The vision telescopes. The sky overhead disappears, replaced by a blackness streaked with lines of cold white, like surgical lamps, or interrogation rooms. In rapid fire, she sees flashes of the places where these people died: a mud-walled room, blood pooled out from a boy's throat; a kitchen, its windows blown out, mother and child curled together under a table; a trench, the ground so saturated with the memory of rain that it is impossible to say where the mud ends and the bodies begin.

Each image is not a memory, but a lived present, hyperreal, the pain of it uncut by time or meaning.

Her chest tightens as if the suffering is a weight.

A child's hand, impossibly small, slides into hers. She glances down; a girl, no older than eight, stares up at her with eyes rimmed in gray. There is a hole in the girl's chest, neat and round, but she stands as if unhurt.

The girl speaks, though her mouth does not move.

It was not by choice. He just did what was told.

Evie tries to respond—who? But the girl is already dissolving, re-placed by the next in the endless queue. Each one leaves behind a fragment: a drop of blood, a torn button, a single word etched into the frost at her feet. She recognizes some words—Russian, Dari, Ara-bic, Serbo-Croatian—but most are just sound, a litany of unfinished business.

The Harbinger watches, somewhere over her left shoulder. Its presence is a shiver in her nervous system, a hunger that wants only to be sated.

Let go, it whispers. Let us hold the pain for you.

She grits her jaw. *No.*

The vision shifts again. Now she is somewhere hot, bright, endless: a desert, the sky a washed-out glare. Cole Danner is here, dressed in digital camo, gun held level at the back of a kneeling man's head. There is no sound, but the violence is absolute. The man does not beg; he just looks up once at Evie, eyes calm, before the gun goes off.

The Harbinger absorbs the blast, ripples of energy passing through Evie's chest, her ribcage vibrating with the echo. Next, Danner stands at the edge of a crater, examining the ruins of a truck, a woman's arm sticking out from underneath. The hand on the arm is adorned with wedding bands. Danner wipes sweat from his brow and moves on.

More flashes: a city street, bodies heaped in the gutter; a motel, plastic shower curtain, red spatter high up the wall; a basement, two men arguing in Russian, one holding a hammer, the other with his hands tied behind his back, head drooping. These deaths are not a soldier doing their duty.

It is endless. A war crimes mixtape, all for her.

She tries to shut it down, to assert control. "It's a construct," she says, to herself or to the Harbinger. "A trauma loop. An intrusive memory, not real."

The Harbinger growls, a wet sound, viscous and ratcheting.

It is real. It is always real.

Still, the Harbinger urges her forward.

Killer.

Evie's rationale rebels. "He's a killer, yes, but so are you. So am I, by proxy."

She feels the pressure now in her chest, a need to act, to resolve the tension. Her hands clench, white-knuckled on the edge of the bench. Sweat beads at her hairline; it runs stinging into her eyes.

And then... nearly weightless paws pad onto her bench.

A wet nose pushes against her palm.

Evie blinks. The world's color returns in a snap; she is on the bench, boots not quite flat to the ground, the taste of iron at her molars. She wipes her face with a jerky motion—when did she start crying?—and looks beside her.

Zork is seated. His coat is a patchwork of ghostly white and brown, unmarred here, as if the mountain's cold has erased all memory of burns. His tail whips once, high and declarative. He nudges again, insistent, and when Evie does not recoil, the little dog hops onto her lap and curls there, a once-living loop of impossible warmth. He's heavier than he looks, and he smells faintly—not of dog, but of rain on new grass, the inside of June's blanket fort, the synthetic lavender of dryer sheets. She presses her face into his fur and tries to inhale back the tears.

The world won't hold still. It jitters at the edges. The warmth against her feels so real. The little body shudders and pulses; his ribcage rises and falls under her hand. She can count the seconds there, feel the little guy's heart.

Evie runs her fingertips over the dog's coat, letting the sensation anchor her.

She looks up, and he is there.

He's taller than she pictured—now with bulk and weight and the immutable density of someone who does not need the world to make room for him. His face is carved in military lines, a map of old scars and careful shaves.

Cole Matthew Danner. Evie has never met him, but she knows... knows by every case she's ever profiled—the vector of death he leaves. He cradles his rifle across his tactical black vest, layered fleece and nylon, winged skull insignia as a patch.

Studying her, Danner stifles down a sly grin. Then nods. "Pretty view, yeah?"

Chapter Twelve

Confrontation Point

The woman on the bench is more rag doll than agent. She's hunched over, hands knotted on her knees, skin papered tight over bone. Her breath ghosts in the air, and her hair—tight little curls—has mostly lost its elasticity. If he cared, Cole might call her a mess. Instead, he catalogs her like everything else: small, female, ethnicity ambiguous but definitely black somewhere in the bloodline, dressed like she expects to die outdoors. Eyes are the giveaway: wide, not with fear, but with a panic that's gone round the bend and come out docile.

He steps into the open, boots loud enough to trigger her. She doesn't flinch.

"Pretty view, yeah?" he says, because it's the sort of inane thing people expect before they're killed.

No response. The woman's jaw flexes. Maybe she's fighting the urge to run, or maybe she's weighing whether she's even worth the bullet.

Cole plants himself three meters out, like he's waiting for a bus. There he can just study her in silence. She's not crying, not talking, not doing much of anything except being extremely present. He counts her breaths, times the blink rate, clocks the slight tremor in her left hand. Could be withdrawal. Might be cold. Could be she's already half-ghost.

He clears his throat. "Name's Cole. You can call me that, if you like." He lets the silence balloon, then: "You out here for the sunset, or just the last bit of oxygen before your lungs stop working?"

The woman straightens. She wipes her mouth with the back of her hand. Her nails are chewed down to the quick. "I was waiting for someone," she says. The voice is even, but with the strain of somebody trying not to say more.

He likes her immediately. "Well, lucky you. Guess I made the appointment." Cole lets his hands hang by his sides. He's never needed to flex to show threat, but for this one, it's probably overkill.

The woman glances at him, then away. "If you're going to kill me, best do it before your partner gets bored."

He laughs. Actually, honest-to-God laughs. "Not a people person, are you?" He gestures with his chin. "I've told you who I am, so why don't you save us both time and tell me who hired you."

She closes her eyes. "Nobody." Pause. "I wasn't hired. I just... needed to come here."

This? This is the point in the job where the mark starts crying, or bargaining, or confessing sins from fifth grade. Instead, the woman gets still, and then does the creepiest thing he's seen all week: she tilts her head, not to him, but to empty space to her left, and mutters, "He's not listening. I doubt they ever listen."

Cole wonders briefly if she's packing a weapon. He's been fooled before, once, by a woman who hid a ceramic razor under her tongue. But this one is wearing the deadness of the truly spent.

He crouches at the edge of the overlook, squints at her in a way that says: you amuse me, but I will still break your spine if you twitch.

"Okay. So, let's say you weren't hired. You came out here for what? The view?" He lets his voice get soft, the way his first-grade teacher used to before pinching ears.

The woman shrugs. "I was told if I sat here long enough, you'd come. Or the other one would. Or Mercer. All roads appear to lead back to him."

"Mercer? Baby, I'm flattered," Cole says, and it is only half a joke. "That's a lot of miles to come just for closure. Hate to disappoint, but the man's not here. Got me instead. You some kind of PI, or...?" He lets the question trail.

She shakes her head. "Profiler. Behavioral Sciences." She sucks in a breath. "Used to be. Doesn't matter now."

Her gaze slides back to the horizon. Something about her silhouette rings a bell—maybe she was on the news once, maybe she's just got one of those faces. He's about to run through his internal Rolodex when the woman says, almost to herself, "How many have you killed?"

Cole puts on his best 'aw shucks' look. "No one keeps count. Not even God."

"I do," she says. Her voice is flat and brittle, like a student reading out a suicide note from the class blackboard. "And so does the Harbinger."

That's a new one. He files it away. "Is that your handler, or just your invisible friend?"

She barks a laugh. The sound of it is too loud, like the first slap after a long silence. "It's a thing. You wouldn't understand. But you're pretty close to its ideal."

Cole leans in, elbow on thigh, like he's settling in for a fireside story. "So enlighten me."

She bites her lip, the left canine digging deep enough to draw a bead of blood. "It kills. That's what it does. But it hates the ones who make killing into an art form. Like you. And Rhys. And Alexei, and all the rest."

Cole smiles, small and mean. "You say it like you're above it. But I see the gun bulge under your left arm."

She doesn't even twitch. "Oh, I know better. I'll never get the chance. That's why I'm here."

Now, this is interesting. Cole rocks back on his heels, satisfied. "So, you think you're going to be the hero. Take down the big, bad mercenary?"

She looks at her own hands. "Not for a moment. I don't think I'm the hero of anything."

It's at this point that he notices the way her right hand keeps stroking near the bench. Not her own thigh, not the wood—she's moving her palm in slow, tender circles. He follows her line of sight and sees nothing. But the way she does it, he's seen that before: it's how the dying touch their pets in the last hours, or the way a kid soothes themselves after the monster leaves the closet.

He lets the silence build. Waits for her to finish.

"You know," he says, "when I was a kid, I used to think people with imaginary friends were just a little broken. Now I realize—" he points two fingers at her head—"it's probably the safest place for anyone you love."

The woman's eyes flick to him. For a second, he thinks she might cry. But instead, she bares her teeth in something that's not a smile.

She says, "You're not afraid of anything, are you?"

"Only boredom." He glances over her shoulder, then raises his voice half a tick: "Rhys, you got her?"

The reply is instantaneous. "Had her for ten minutes, boss. She's all yours."

The woman closes her eyes.

Cole sighs. It's always like this: his big build, their trembling, the wait for the kill. But this one is... disappointing. He expected more. A hidden blade, a hail-Mary play, some last-minute bargaining. Instead, all he gets is a woman too tired to care, talking to ghosts and petting an invisible dog.

He stands. "This should be the part where I ask if you have any last words, but I don't think you'd bother."

She shakes her head.

He wants to savor it, but there's nothing left to savor. This isn't a job. It's a mercy kill.

He un-holsters his Desert Eagle, lets it hang loose in his grip. The thing is so large; it looks like a cartoon in his hand. He pulls the slide back with a practiced flick, the round chambering with a loud, oily click.

"I'm probably doing you a favor," he says, and means it.

She doesn't even look up.

Chapter Thirteen

Local Advantage

The Marriott conference room is understandably less sterile now. Afternoon light finds the seams in the blackout curtains, highlighting every flaw in the wood veneer. The table is a spread of crime scene pics and legal pads. Liam can't help but notice Cassandra off on her end of the charging cables, so enwrapped by her laptop and digital detective stuff.

He prefers the far side, flanked by a whiteboard and an old-school carafe of coffee. Proper means. The others—Marcus Vaughn and Elena Reyes—are clustered mid-table, passing a single printout between them.

Cassandra rises in her seat, pushing her glasses up, then back at her notes. "I think I've got something." She taps the laptop. "There's a partial destination on the last truck renewal. Local. I've mapped the address."

Marcus leans in. "How partial?"

"I've got the number, street and city." Webb drags her finger along the grain of the desk. "It's a condo community, but—" She flicks to the screen. "—the 'unit' line is blank. Probably intentionally so."

Reyes pipes up, "Or an Airbnb that he didn't get until he picked up the check-in instructions."

Webb nods. "That'd be my guess too. But until we get a search warrant for the host data, we'll be stalled for a good day or two. That's if we get a judge who likes us."

Hayes gets up to spy on the map for himself. He knows the place. Midtown, new construction, the kind of condos that market as 'urban luxury' and then fill with business travelers or short-term renters. He rubs his jaw, the stubble catching on his palm. Despite being tired, the puzzle pulls him in. "We could go down in person. That sort of building's got a front-desk person after five. Maybe one of my guys may know them."

Marcus scoffs. "Sure, there's no mistrust of feds here."

"Suits, yes." Hayes shrugs. "Sheriffs, not so much. It's worked before."

Haden, who's been quiet so long Hayes thought he might have slipped out, says, "You think he left anything behind?"

Hayes meets the old profiler's gaze. "If our guy was operating solo, he might not have known he'd be dead in a week. Most perps assume they've got another night, one more meal, etcetera."

Agent Haden leans back, the chair creaking. He steeples his hands, then drops them to the table. "How soon can you get your Sheriffs over there?"

Hayes doesn't hesitate. "If we go now, we'll catch the afternoon shift at changeover. I've pulled favors for less."

Marcus frowns. "And if we stride in while they're conducting their interviews?"

"At least we won't be the first in. Neighbors get curious, is all. They'd likely want to help a beat cop rather than men-in-black. Sorry, ladies." Liam deferred to Cass and Reyes. "If we happen to spot evidence of a crime while we're there, then it's a fresh call for search and seizure." He takes a breath. "We can't afford to let this get any colder."

A brittle silence hangs for a beat.

Cassandra breaks first. "If no one else volunteers, my legs could use the stretch." She looks up, eyes bright.

Reyes is already packing her laptop. "How much backup you need?"

Liam shakes his head. "I just need someone to vouch for the federal angle. In case anyone asks."

Marcus stands, checking his sidearm. "Let's not lose momentum. I'll ride along. You know, in case things go sideways."

Haden makes the smallest of nods. "You have a point, Detective. Anything you find, you report directly. Marcus, we'll regroup here afterward. Everyone needs to stay sharp and in the loop."

Liam notes the slight deflation in Cass and Reyes. Guess this Marcus guy has the seniority. Despite that, there's an unexpected warmth in Liam's chest. He's worked with the Bureau before, but usually as the token local. Today feels sort of... different.

He tucks the address slip into his jacket, grabs his keys, and signals to Marcus. They walk out together.

Liam is content simply to drive, with Marcus occupying the shotgun position. His assigned partner taps on the armrest in time to a song only he hears. The city outside lulls into a late autumn light, going gold with the shadows stretching out. They cruise through high-rise canyons, past coffee shops and glass-front gyms.

Arriving at the condo complex, a few Sheriff's cruisers are wedged at the curb. Hayes recognizes one in the lobby—Chambers, a guy who's usually first to take extra shifts. He flashes the patrolman a two-finger wave. Chambers buzzes them in.

In under a half-hour, they've canvassed the complex. While most KC locals were friendly enough, a few Show-me'ers were even more so. Chambers pocketed a couple of phone numbers from the more eligible neighbors because of his crisp uniform. As fortune has it, Blanche, the owner of the unit they were searching for is also a resident. Having law enforcement enquiring made her more than eager to afford them a look/see.

With the turn of a key, Liam cautions Blanche to hold back while their deputies inspected. And with that...

They're in.

The place is staged like a typical rental: pale gray carpet, modular furniture, framed abstract art on the walls. It's so clean, it's almost a negative space. Hayes steps inside, letting his senses map the room. He follows the carpet to the kitchen.

There's a smell, faint but familiar: bleach and plastics. He turns, scans the counters and sees on the floor a length of blue plastic sheeting, rolled tight and taped at the ends. Pulling on gloves, Hayes is careful not to disturb anything.

Marcus circles behind him, eyes alert. "Well, seems like our perp. Probably his packing is done here, too."

Hayes nods.

Under the sink, a box of latex gloves, two bottles of Betadine, and a half-empty container of industrial-strength hydrogen peroxide. The fridge is empty except for bottled water. The freezer, though, holds a surprise: tucked at the back, a disposable cold pack, the kind used for shipping perishables, and beside it, a small white cooler.

Marcus puts on gloves, then cracks the cooler. Empty, but he sniffs—flinches back and tightens his eyes a beat. Tipping forward, the interior is stained yellow, as if iodine had been wiped up, but not entirely.

Hayes stands back, taking in the wider scene. Logic clicks into place, the way a puzzle's last piece just fits in and you know the picture is settled. *Yeah. He's right.* Turning to his partner, Liam says, "We should check the dumpsters."

Marcus goes, returning a moment later with a plastic evidence bag. Inside: a scrap of cardboard box, the kind that ships high-end medical devices. The label has been scored out with a Sharpie, but the outline of the letters is still visible: OCS—Organ Care System.

"Well," Marcus says, deadpan. "Now we know how they carried the heart out."

Hayes grunts. "Let's photo everything. I'll call in a local evidence tech."

They work the scene for the next forty minutes, cataloging every item, every trace, every place where human error may have left a fingerprint. Marcus finds a few stray hairs in the bathroom sink. Thankfully, they're not tight curls. He smartly leaves them for forensics to bag and tag.

With the sun below the skyline and the windows burnishing orange, Marcus sits at the little dining table and stares out. It's a familiar look: his case is building itself inside his head, every new data point adding weight to his hypothesis.

Hayes settles in across from him.

Vaughn is tired, but not in the same way as this morning. Now it's the tired of a man who knows he's getting somewhere. Without looking back... "You know, back at the Bureau, they used to say that if you're chasing ghosts, it's because you don't want to find the living."

Hayes nods, allowing his words to land.

Marcus leans in, voice softer. "I'm curious? What are you hoping to find here, Detective?"

There is a tone to his question—an implied one. Hayes draws a long breath and turns to the dusk light creeping across the room. Evie is out there somewhere, chasing the same lines but farther ahead. This is his job, of course. But is he building a case against her, or just trying to salvage what's left?

Liam doesn't have an answer for Marcus, so he waves him off.

Both resigning themselves, they rise to document the rest of the details. Forensics arrives for the collection, and relieves them of the remaining responsibilities.

In the lobby, the condo-owner is waiting, a different smile this time: more wary, less certain she wants to know what's upstairs. Hayes slips the pink seizure order into Blanche's palm, saying, "We'll need to keep the unit under lock until forensics is done. Apologies for the loss of rent in the interim." He tries a half-smile, but it dies in the cold air of the lobby.

Outside, the air has turned sharp, a warning of winter to come. Marcus has already situated himself in the passenger seat of the sedan. Hayes tosses his notes into the back and climbs in behind the wheel. They got what they came for: answers, confirmation—a 'right track.'

But now what?

With a turn of the key, the engine starts. The dashboard glows to life.

Hayes and Vaughn head back to the Marriott, to the conference room with its war zone of files, faces and coffee.

Chapter Fourteen

Easier Said

She doesn't flinch, cower, or beg for the half-second he might grant her. Instead, she's vacant, off in some trance. Her mouth moves, lips stitched tight, whispering nothings to the space beside her. There's no thrill in this.

Cole cocks his head.

He takes two steps back and looks over the edge. The river is five hundred vertical feet below their little scenic overlook, a drop so sheer it'd be inevitable. He could save himself a bullet. She's got nowhere to go. If she fought, it'd be over before the sound reached the tree line. How else would it look but suicide?

His voice comes out weirdly gentle. "Hello, miss? Anything else to say?"

She doesn't lift her head. Just keeps oddly kneading at the space before her. That's when it hits him, an uncoiling in the pit of his stomach. The churn one gets before an op goes sideways, when the room is just a little too silent before the flashbang. He looks closer at the way her hand moves—slow, rhythmic, not nervous but deliberate.

There's almost a lump in the small of her lap. He follows her arm, down and to the left. Down... and to the left. A memory of a dog rises in the air. Its... light milkiness, a clean dander and...

In the twitch of an eye, he sees it: tiny paws coming into focus, the panting breaths, tail wagging—reddening cracked burn scars.

That goddamn Jack Russell.

It is half-made of light, half shadow, eyes like marbles with the sky caught inside. The dog sits there in her lap, unblinking, tongue lolling. The surrounding cold sharpens, the temperature dropping three degrees.

Cole's bravado vanishes in a gasp. He saw it die. Remembers the howls. He'd laughed. So had Rhys. They thought it was damn funny, the way the stupid bastard wouldn't jump from the window. Now here it is, staring up at him.

He lifts the Desert Eagle, aiming for the woman's head, but his hand shakes. The wind kicks up, but there is no sound. The dog's jaw opens, showing a mouthful of perfect white teeth. It smiles.

Her eyes come up to meet his. Where soft brown had been, there is now only jet black, two pits sucking up the light and a distant seething cold within them.

The world shifts around him, as if gravity has doubled for everything but him. The space before the woman thickens; the bench cracks under the strain. The ghost dog's form smears, like a shadow melting, wrapping around her waist and up her side. Her body jerks rigid, a puppet with taunt strings. Lips part, and a sound comes out—a vibration more than a word. It drills into Cole's jawbone and ricochets behind his teeth. Ethereal wisps coalesce around her form.

And the Harbinger lunges.

Cole doesn't remember dropping his guns, but they're gone. The Harbinger's distended hands close around his throat, burning in like liquid nitrogen. His muscular body's weight builds on his clenched neck. He tries to punch, to twist, but without the ground beneath his feet there is no leverage. The air fills with the stink of cordite, dog breath and a wet, metallic tang that could only be fear, his own... and yet not his own.

It speaks: not in language, but in memory of every act he ever laughed off. His vision splits, and in the instant before he decides fight-or-flight...

Time stops.

He is five years old, being held underwater by his brother, the moment of panic stretched out into a lifetime. Cole is twenty-seven, waking up in a Turkish bathhouse, the bodies around him cooling fast, and the one survivor looking at him with accusation. He is thirty-nine, his own hands pressed to the base of a hooker's skull, the thrill of the snap and the regret that it didn't last longer.

The Harbinger lifts him, not just his body but the entirety of his being. He's off the ground, boots dangling, the cliff's edge back there. The seated woman remains below him, hands in her lap, looking up. The eyes are black and blacker, infinite and deep.

She says, "You know what comes next."

And he does. Of course he does. He's always known.

The Harbinger's grip tightens; every nerve in his body screams. He gropes for his knife, but his hand isn't there. He's not sure if it's gone or if he's just lost the will to feel it.

Far below, the river calls. The sound is a roar, but it is not water—it is the gathering crowd of those silenced, every plea, every "don't" and "please." They're all down there, waiting for him. It's like a wide-open grave with a bed of victims to welcome him back.

The Harbinger hauls him past the lip. From the periphery, Cole sees the edge grow farther from hope. Then pause. For a heartbeat, the world is nothing but wind and sky and the vacuum of what he's never been able to feel. Then its grip... releases.

He falls.

Time is meaningless now. Seconds stretch out into meters, then into miles, then into the years he spent running from the thing he's only just now meeting.

It is pointless for him to close his eyes, for the wind peels them open. His throat is raw. He wants to scream, but he's out of breath and out of his mind.

Cole plummets.

Just another body for the earth.

River rocks are coming up finally. He braces for the pain, but the Harbinger knows mercy of another sort. It stretches out the moment before, makes him see the possible, every path he has chosen. When his victims receive him, they pass him along, each one digging in with claws and teeth and hunger. Pieces of Cole shear off, shreds of memory, rents of skin, the self-importance, the confidence, his last measure of denial. He wants to say, "I'm sorry," but there's no one left to say it to. There is only an echo of the Harbinger's laughter, ringing the last few feet... inches... infinite fractions of a second.

He smacks the granite like wet meat. Every bone shatters. The pain is cosmic.

There is nothing but black—black—black, and the last thing he feels is the tongue of a dog licking his face, cold and wet, yet still forgiving.

Then he's gone.

Chapter Fifteen

Incredulous

For a moment, the world stands so perfectly still that Rhys Fitz wonders if he's suffered a hallucinatory seizure—some silent, total-system arrest from the sight of Cole Danner yanked off his feet by pure, predatory air.

One instant, Cole's boots are squared on the overlook; next, he's vertical, arms snapping up like he's the butt of a cosmic joke. Then the impossible: he rises, six inches, a foot, a body's length, higher. His mouth is open. No sound. The wind should be screaming, but there's only the sharp, wet hush of the river, somewhere far below.

That woman on the bench—whoever she is—doesn't even turn. She just sits there while Cole flails in space, the big bastard's limbs working the air like a marionette, all his size and training amounting to nothing.

Rhys squints through his Leupold scope, expecting a harness, a wire trick, anything he can process. Instead, the sight jumps, blurs, as if the glass itself can't stand the vision. Cole is jerking now, feet bicycling, a puppet in unseen hands. Then, abruptly, he's hurled sideways, thirty meters east, rag-dolling over the void. For a fraction of a second, Cole's head snaps toward the tree line and their eyes lock, even at this distance. There's nothing left of the man but shock. Then gravity retakes him, and he plummets, out of frame.

Simply gone.

A thought rolls out of Rhys' mouth. "If I didn't see that myself, I'd call me a liar."

He sucks in a breath, resetting his world. *Check your perimeter, Fitz.* When things go weird, check your goddamn perimeters. He plants his elbows, blinks out the afterimage, and scopes the bench again. The woman hasn't moved. Rhys lines up the crosshairs on the base of her skull—the squeeze is already halfway done before his training interrupts:

Don't.

That's not the mission. You're supposed to determine who she is, who sent her.

But the mission is up in the wind, or falling to splinter on rocks far below. If Cole's out, Rhys is on his own, and this situation—whatever it is—just went from off-book to off-world.

He sights again, dragging his pulse down to a sniper's three-count.

One: crosshairs steady, target seated like she damn-well wants to be shot.

Two: exhale, prep for recoil, feel the gentle tension on the trigger.

Three:—

Icy fingers run up his spine. Not a metaphorical shiver—an actual, literal, freezing crawl, as if someone's rakes the inside of his vertebrae with popsicle fingers. Rhys jerks off the scope, spins, and claps a palm to the back of his neck.

Nothing.

He glances about. Pine shadows, long and thin in the afternoon, nothing moving except a patch of breeze. He sets the Dragunov aside and stretches his back. "Get a grip, Fitz. Christ's sake."

But the cold doesn't leave. It spreads—a slow, hypodermic leak into his lungs.

Panting, he wraps his hands around the barrel, grounding himself in the metal's reality, the polish and the weight and the little dings from old, unfunny nights. He whips his head around, scans the tree line.

And the world is wrong.

Not the trees, nor the ground, not his vantage; all those are mapped and remembered. But the shadows are... not behaving. They creep up the hill, curl in wrong directions, pulse out of sync with the sun. For a second, his eyes must be going—the first, ugly symptom of a TIA or some rare nerve agent. But then the cold stabs deeper, and now there are shapes among the trunks. Not the play of wind or the dash of critters—actual, walking shapes, inhumanly thin, traipsing through the pines.

Rhys cycles the bolt, checks the scope. The world goes monochrome. He brings the Dragunov back to his cheek, glassing their approach.

The shapes have faces.

He recognizes the first immediately—a woman in a parka, one eye swollen shut, the left cheek a ruin of purple and blue. She moves toward him with the same mechanical persistence she'd had on the day she died, pushing through snowdrifts to beg for mercy. She'd perish on the Balkans job, heard the last air crawl from her throat. The memory was a scar. Now she's a reality, less than forty feet away.

"No." He lowers the scope. "No way in hell."

The next figure is a man, balding, heavyset, with a streak of red across his collarbone. Russian. The one who screamed Rhys's name as they broke his legs in the cellar. Behind him, a girl with a crooked jaw and an arm bent at an unnatural angle—her hair matted with blood.

All of them walking uphill toward his sniper's nest. Their eyes are not accusatory, not even angry; they're empty, the look of those who want only to close the loop.

Rhys grabs for the sidearm at his thigh, yanks it free. "Stay back!" he shouts, but the words dissolve into the hush. He fires twice—pop, pop—the slugs tearing through the woman's chest, dusting the parka with vapor. She doesn't slow. The Russian grins, and his lips split along an old, familiar seam. The child at the rear cocks her head, then launches into a sprint.

Rhys backpedals, boots churning mud, rifle swinging wide for a melee he's never trained for. He's seen death—hundreds of times, in countless variations—but never like this.

These nightmares are coming for him in broad daylight!

He lobs the Dragunov at the Russian, grabs for his bugout pack, and bolts. Trees whip past, branches scratch his face, but he never loses the sense of them behind: woman, man, child, and every other name and body he's ever put into a shallow grave. They don't follow fast, but they are not stopping. Every time he looks back, the numbers have grown. A boy with a hole in his throat. The bearded man missing both hands. A blonde, naked to the waist, skin charred black from the C-4 trap he'd set.

The cold is in his marrow now, a syrupy drag on his heart. Rhys veers through the trees, instincts reverting to pure survival. If he can just keep ahead, just put a little ground between him and the dead, he can—

He slams into a wall of air, rebounding off it hard. The snow is suddenly three feet deep. How? It was bare ground up here. Rhys claws himself upright, fingers raw, eyes darting for an escape. But the clearing is full, every gap between trees jammed with the dead. They press forward, faces crowding in. A dozen eyes, all fixed on him.

Then something else moves in from behind.

It arrives not as a person, but as a smear—a negative, a subtraction of color and matter, a moving wound through the air. It flows around the edges of the crowd, picking up bits of their loss as it goes, until it towers above, all writhing mist and the suggestion of teeth.

The eyes are hatred distilled to a vector.

Rhys's mind tunnels. There's no logic in this, no tactic, no clever twist. The only path is through, and he is not the one making the rules.

He clamps his mouth shut, squeezes his eyelids together, and thinks of every war story he's ever heard—how men died well, how they kept secrets to the end, how they didn't break. He tries to conjure Cole's face, that last split-second of terror, the floating body, the shriek, his drop.

But it's all for nothing.

The woman in the parka leans in, presses her frozen lips to his cheek, "We're gone," then whispers, "but not forgotten."

The Harbinger surges, slamming through their spirits, through the man, through the child, and buries itself in Rhys Fitz's skull. The cold is absolute. His vision fractures, then shatters.

In the last instant—another voice rings out, clear and true: "No!"

It is the woman. Her word is a command.

"Not like this."

Rhys's world jerks.

He finds himself on his hands and knees, palms seared, breath pouring out of him in thick gasps. He sags, forehead pressed into the moss and ice, and begins to sob—hard, fast, without shame.

There's no one left to see.

The next few seconds are missing. Rhys reboots into existence hunched behind a deadfall, the taste of bile in his mouth and a hollow ring in his ears. The snow is gone again—how?—and he's shivering in ordinary, rational cold, the kind that comes from almost dying in the mountains.

The woman stands above him.

Her boots are planted at his head, but she doesn't move to touch him or even acknowledge his gasping panic. She's braced, knees locked, every muscle straining as if she's fending off a seizure. Her arms hang at her sides, fists trembling. In the pale light of late afternoon, she's the most alive thing in the world.

Rhys blinks, spits out dirt.

She inhales—once, twice, three times, each breath a fight. Her mouth opens, lips blue, and hears the tiniest whimper. It's like the mewling of a trapped animal. Then she sets her jaw and swallows hard.

The air thickens. Not just with cold, but with something else—a pressure that makes Rhys's gums ache. For a second he's certain his teeth will pop out, one by one, as if someone's using slow-motion pliers on his skull.

"That's enough." The woman speaks, but not to him: "We're done here. I'm not doing this."

The world around Rhys tunnels. At the fringes, something wavers, an oily vague ether—no longer outside, no longer hunting. It slips closer to the woman, threads itself through her coat and skin, seeping under her collar.

She shudders and straightens.

In that second, his world becomes possible again. Sunlight returns. The cold is only cold.

Rhys breathes, and with the breath comes a flush of hope: It's over. The nightmare's ended. He remains a survivor, and with survivors comes the privilege of stories, of commiseration, of finding a bar someday and telling the tale to another old killer who might even believe him.

He laughs. It's a raw, animal sound, too high in the throat to be manly, but it's still laughter.

She turns to him, eyes wet but unafraid.

He tries to say, 'Thanks.' But his syllables tumble out in a slurry.

Raising her head back, her nostrils flare. She sneers down at him. Well then screw her then. Guess she didn't want his gratitude. The woman's cheek trembles with held-back rage as she manages to step back and turn away.

Her breathing sounds forced, measured—willing herself calm as her footsteps over needles and twigs grows more distant.

Rhys closes his eyes, savoring the relief, the sensation of a body that hurts for reasons he understands. Then he opens them again.

That's when the crowd reappears.

He sees the faces—scores of them, layered and stacked, a terraced amphitheater of the dead. Some are just impressions, smudges of personality; others are sharp as razors, so clear he could draw them from memory.

They do not move. They do not breathe. But their eyes are all on him.

Rhys stumbles to his feet, legs jelly, and staggers backward. The amphitheater of dead watches, impassive, as he flails and slips, landing on his back. He expects them to close in, to finish the job. He looks at the woman.

She's paused now. Back to him and still, some fifty yards away.

The dead crowd moves, one deliberate, silent step at a time. They flow past him in procession. First, the woman in the parka, she drags a glistening wet hand across his scalp. Her suffering takes root. Behind her stride up the rest, each a distinct language of death and mutilation. Their numbers grow, a parade of the dead, the wronged, and the collateral damage. Each one brings their own cargo of regret, their own cut of memory, and with every new arrival Rhys's brain fills, crowding out the present, stuffing him with the person he is and the person he can never undo.

His scream is weak, and he can't tell if he's making it with his mouth or only inside his skull.

At some point, his world goes dark. The wind rattles the pines. Rhys lies curled, sobbing, then laughing, then just muttering, a slow, recursive loop of nothing.

Chapter Sixteen

Balancing Act

Her soul could withstand only so much. Evie doesn't so much draw a line as yank back on it instead. Her limit becomes its leash.

Resistance does not come gently.

The core of her being hurtles against the Harbinger's vengeful momentum. Like being thrown from a moving train—one moment every cell in her body is alight with a certainty, the next she is unceremoniously dumped back into her own body. Visions of what the Harbinger had done... what it was about to do, rebounds from the spiritual impact.

For a few beats, she stands there, letting her breathing come back under her control. Her tongue tastes of a burnt bitterness, and her eyes ache from tears she can't recall shedding.

A hundred feet off, the other sniper is sprawled on the ground. He's not dead, nor even unconscious—his boots scuff at the dirt, his chest heaves in ugly, arrhythmic shudders. Every few breaths, he emits a strangled half-laugh, then a gulping moan. If he is aware of her, it doesn't show.

Evie watches him for a full minute, trying to summon pity, or hatred, or anything specific. Instead, she feels the most hollow thing in the world: relief.

She stopped it.

Stopped herself.

Stopped the Harbinger before it could devour another and leave her even more diminished. And if that meant a ruined man writhing in dirt, well... she stopped expecting the world had proportional returns a while ago.

Evie wipes her mouth, and checks for blood. Her hands tremble, right thumb jerking in micro-seizures. She counts to three, willing them to stop.

The mountain air is sharp enough to cut skin. She pulls the scarf up to her chin, letting it mask the shivering. Then, with a steadying breath, she walks to where the contractor is flopped, clutching his own shoulders in a fetal response.

She crouches beside him, boots in crusted snow.

"Hey," she says, aiming for calm but missing by a notch. "Look at me."

He keeps his eyes screwed shut. His lips quiver, teeth clicking a staccato. A ripped hole is growing at the knee of his tactical pants.

"Surprise. You're not dead." She grips him. "Still, I'm not going to leave you here either."

At the sound of her voice, there's a recognition, followed by a gasp. He tries to scuttle backward, but his body won't obey. The soldier opens one eye, then the other, each with a wince.

Evie will have to shoulder whatever is left of this one.

Stumbling out of the woods, the heft of this lumbering dirtbag is almost more than she cares to bear, but Evie perseveres all the same. She crosses the glade and staggers her way to the main entrance. Its entry stanchion sits before the door—a thick slab of carbon fiber, inset with a retinal scanner and a small, discreet call box. Evie presses the button. The response is instant, almost eager: "State your name and medical emergency."

She tilts her face to the camera, lets the system take her in. "I have your man here. Severe mental trauma. He needs immediate attention."

A pause, then: "Do you have weapons?"

Evie pulls her coat aside, showing the Glock. "I'm not looking to invade. As far as I'm concerned, this is more of a garbage dump."

Another pause. Then the door unseals with a pneumatic hiss, opening into a foyer of white tile and artificial light. Three people rush forward: two in medical scrubs, one in a blazer with an ID badge clipped to the lapel. The lead medic—a short, efficient woman with close-cropped hair—reaches for the contractor. He collapses into her arms. Lowering him onto a gurney, and before she can say anything else, a nurse applies a patch to his neck.

Within seconds, his body slackens, his eyes flutter, and he sags inert.

The blazer approaches Evie, wary but professional. "Did you find him like this?"

She shakes her head. "Tried to kill me. It didn't go his way." Evie considers her next words, then says it anyway. "He's seen things. Done things. Things he can never undo... or unsee. If I were you, I'd keep him sedated until you get a real psychiatrist on-site. Not just a house shrink—a real one. Either way, he's your mess now."

With a spin of the gurney, they wheel him back into the facility. Their door's seal behind them, hissing the world out.

Silence returns. Evie's emptiness creeps back, the kind that isn't about killers or ghosts or even justice. It is just fatigue, raw and elemental.

She stops at the edge of the driveway, boots planted in the half-melted snow. From here, she can see the whole compound: the mirrored windows. It is beautiful in a way—perfectly insulated, nothing getting in unless allowed.

Her hands are steady now. The tremor is gone. She looks up at the sky, checks her wrist for the time—habit, not hope.

But.

There was the tracker. Its path led her here. Mercer's people are methodical; they must have discovered it when they unboxed the heart. Which means they'd have relocated the payload—brought the box here as bait. Makes sense.

However, it wasn't just about bringing her here. *Was it?* This place was a solution to a problem. One they'd expect resolved by this time. Even more likely, it was also about directing attention away from where it was originally intended. Mercer was never here.

She affords herself a smile.

Turning from the building, Evie checks her pockets for the car keys. She finds them, gloved and cold, and starts down the winding drive toward the forest, toward the ditch she had hidden her battered Ford.

She keeps her pace slow at first. If one moves too fast after a trauma, something always gets left behind. A mile of forest and switchbacks waits between her and her ride out. Hands jammed in her pockets, she works the problem. Mercer recognized a threat to his operation when the tracker was discovered. He relied on his top operatives to ensure it was taken care of, far from anywhere that would point back to him. Now, those operatives are off the game board. That makes the next move hers.

As she walks, the weight of what she's done tugs at her, but it is a familiar burden. Today, she could find some sense of mercy. Tomorrow, she may not have that luxury.

She is still here.

And she knows where to go.

Some rich bastard took her family, and shoved them face-first through hell. She needs to know why. Who murdered her daughter? Where is her body? Evie wants answers—to know the truth. She doesn't want bloodshed; her June deserves justice.

That's on Mercer now.

One way or another, she'll damn well get it.

Chapter Seventeen

Circumstantial Evidence

Haden likes to think that nothing in the world smells like an FBI war room, but the truth is, he's been in enough to know: the scent is always the same. Burned coffee, too-hot laptops, and a current of stress-sweat that floats above even the best HVAC. The space in this Marriott is no different, so thick with recycled breath and caffeine that the only way to stay awake is to keep moving.

He does laps along the window, letting the others work the evidence pile. In the last twelve hours, their case has spun itself into a full category five: organ theft, international victim, a missing heart and—because the Bureau loves a callback—a new string of data points that keep curving back to Evelyn damned Cross.

Haden floats behind Cass's left shoulder, reading upside-down as she toggles between two PDFs. The first is the official autopsy, top-lined with the kind of bureaucratic euphemism that makes Haden want to swallow glass: "Unusual Circumstances, Cause of Death:

Exsanguination due to Thoracic Trauma." The second is a high-res scan of the ME's notes, annotated with Cassandra's own tight script.

Not bothering to look up, Cass says, "We've confirmed it was the aortic root. Whoever did this, they had to cut through the pericardium and clamp off the great vessels. You see these?" She points with her pen. "It appears they used some V-shaped wedge, then widened it with blunt force. You can see the secondary trauma here, and here."

Vaughn grunts. "You're saying it was a two-person job?"

"Not necessarily. But definitely not your average kitchen butcher," Cass responds.

Hayes, standing over her, squints at the photo. "That's a lot of muscle to pop the sternum. You ever see a woman do that?"

Webb shakes her head, but not in a way that says she's convinced. "Strength, sure. But it's not impossible. The technique is more important than the brawn. I mean, give me a large enough lever and I can move the world."

Vaughn can't help himself. "So, if it's a girl, she had a handy car jack. Got it."

Hayes rolls his eyes, but he doesn't let it go. "Evie's what, five-one? She'd have to climb on top of the guy. Or have help."

Cassandra's tone stays glacial. "Statistically speaking, women in organ trafficking are more likely to play support roles, not direct extraction. But then, when it comes to Evie and statistics, she always gravitates toward the outlier points."

Haden moves to the coffee, pours himself a cup, then stands next to Reyes. She mutters, "You think she did this?" Not loud enough for the room, but for him alone.

He sips. "I think she's capable of anything she sets her mind to."

Reyes nods, then turns back to her phone.

Vaughn flips through the photos and fans out a set of four. "Check this. Blood spatter at the scene. Either it was done fast, or someone who wanted to make it look fast did it. Not to mention the whole bloody thing was done without a single footprint."

Detective Hayes says, "Seems more like a show. But then what's the message?"

Cassandra slides Haden the annotated ME report. "You want my honest answer? I'd say whoever did it was not familiar with surgical procedure. And not just the cut. While there was care taken to sever the blood flow from the heart cleanly, the surrounding tissue was utterly brutalized. It's like all they wanted was the heart."

Liam shakes his head, the skepticism solid in his voice. "I may just be a local yokel detective, but you're all talking like Evie is Hannibal Lecter with a doctorate in engineering. I just don't buy it. There's got to be another angle."

Cassandra adds, "Sometimes the simplest answer—"

Vaughn cuts her off. "Is the one you can't prove in court."

Hayes leans forward, sliding his elbows across the table. "Let's talk about the size. Volkov was six feet, two-fifty. That guy is not going down easy. So what, Evie walks in and—what, chloroforms him? Hits him with a brick?"

Webb shrugs. "No evidence of either. Maybe he trusted her. Maybe she didn't do it alone."

Hayes cocks her an eye. "You people have worked with Evie before, right? Does any of that sound remotely plausible?"

They let that hang. All eyes drift to Haden.

He feels the pressure, but refuses to blink. "If she's teamed up, we'll know soon enough. There's always a leak."

Vaughn is visibly enjoying the tension. "Might not be Evie at all. Maybe she's being set up."

Webb counters, "But she was there. Cameras caught her at the airport."

"Circumstantial," Marcus says, "unless you want to bet the entire case on a blurred security photo. Remember the last time we tried to sell purely circumstantial evidence to a judge?"

"She didn't even try to hide," Reyes replies. "Maybe she wanted us to see her."

Haden says, "Or she wanted someone else to know she was in play."

Vaughn grins. "Now we're thinking like profilers."

Hayes let out a huff. "Then who's she chasing?"

An old ache radiates behind Haden's eye. He rubs at it, working the knot. "That's what we need to figure out. Let's work the timeline. Volkov enters the country on a fake passport, rents a truck, zig-zags the South for ten months, always a new condo, always cash. He shows up in Kansas City, tries to turn himself in, ends up dead on a slab, heartless. Cross is in the area. So what's her objective?"

Webb says, "If it's not revenge, maybe she's spying for some lead?"

Vaughn nods. "She's hunting the next link up the chain. If Volkov was on a leash, who's his handler?"

Reyes, quietly, "Or the recipient."

A cold, greasy thread of anxiety worms into Haden's gut. He knows this flavor. It's the taste of a case turning into something bigger than the Bureau. If the Russian angle holds, it'll escalate from his team to the feds-with-a-capital-F. The moment it goes international, it's out of his hands.

No. That's not going to happen.

Fueling his lungs with oxygen, he turns back to his team. "I want everything on Volkov's contacts. There's a reason we don't have his phone. Find it and every signal he ever pinged. If there's a handler, I want a name. And keep running down Cross—if she's looking for something, she's going to make a move. We need to get ahead of her. If she thinks this is her case, we're about to show her how wrong she is."

They nod, but the fatigue is visible on every face. Webb closes her laptop with a soft click. Reyes flops back into her chair. Vaughn checks his phone, then pockets it. Even Detective Hayes looks wrung out.

Haden waits until they've dispersed, then walks to the window and stares out at the parking lot. The lights outside make everything flat and jaundiced. For a second, he allows himself to feel the weight of it: Cross is out there, running her own play; his team is on edge; and behind it all, the certainty that this story is about to turn darker.

He pulls out his phone, thumbs the screen, and scrolls until he finds her number. He hesitates. There's a protocol to this—an entire book of Bureau rules that says he should not, under any circumstances, reach out to a person of interest in an active case.

He does it anyway.

The text is short, almost flippant:

HADEN: If you're running surveillance, let me back you up. If you're going rogue, tell me why.

Chapter Eighteen

The Unanswered Call

Evie picks the motel for its angle: a raw sightline to every entry and egress off the state highway, the open corridor curling around so she can monitor her Fiesta. Nobody's going to catch her off guard tonight. June's scarf is drawn up to her chin; she uses it less for the cold than for her scent.

Her phone has service. She's not sure she likes it.

There's a message waiting.

> HADEN: If you're running surveillance, let me back you up. If you're going rogue, tell me why.

A beat. Then another.

No follow-up. Which means he's waiting for her to show her cards first.

She powers the phone off, slides it under the mattress. Evie stands and walks the room perimeter, back and forth. She wants to feel like a wolf on patrol, but mostly it seems like a zoo specimen, all potential and no action.

Her stomach growls. She waits for it to pass, but it doesn't, so she slings up her pack and drags herself to the parking lot.

She's already three blocks down, at a diner with a sign that reads "ALWAYS OPEN, ALWAYS FRESH," before she recognizes her need for noise to mask the static in her head.

Evie finds a booth to collapse into. The server is a middle-aged woman with a name tag, and the other patrons are a line of long-haul drivers and two retirees running a chess game as quietly as possible. Perfect. Just what she needs to go along with a water and a BLT.

The place is wall-to-wall mirrors and plastic. Great for seeing who's watching whom, bad for pretending you're invisible.

Evie flops out her ThinkPad, boots into the secure partition, and calls up the folder labeled ETHOS. All her best and worst ideas are stocked here. She hesitates, fingers over the keys, then splits the screen to show the satellite overlays of Mercer's airstrip compound. The place where her tracker originally landed. She zooms and pans and double-checks the images, annotating with notes which only make sense to her.

She toggles over to the ETHOS chat. HeapMonk is online, as is RootMuse. CtrlZ, their ringleader, displays his glitchy/clean avatar. Their names crawl with pop-ups.

CTRLZ: Diner WiFi, Evie? Really?

EVIE: Tor / VPN triple onion. No SSID leakage. Am I burning?

ROOTMUSE: Only the cheese. You've got more threats from the cardiac end than SIG-INT.

EVIE: At least I'm still here.

ROOTMUSE: HeapMonk nearly had a coronary after you disconnected. Thought you'd been bagged.

HEAPMONK: Thought you were dead.

EVIE: Not dead. Just lightly exorcized.

EVIE: They'd left a trap for me to walk into. Were not expecting my borderline short-stuff approach. At least they had no idea who I was.

She leans on her elbow and types one-handed, feeling her pulse hop under the skin. Evie replays the memory of the clinic, the Harbinger humming over the needled ground. The way that contractor's eyes bugged, how his mouth worked soundlessly before falling into the ravine.

EVIE: It didn't work out so well for them. But I certainly learned where Mercer was not.

HEAPMONK: Was it the ones that came after me?

She lets her hands rest on the keyboard, flattening her fingers against the plastic like she could press the world into a simpler topology. The taste of the wind from the overlook lingers—metallic, electric.

The part of her that should feel guilt is strangely blank, a smooth erased field. Nothing to do but keep moving.

> EVIE: Yes.

She closes her eyes. The memory surfaces, not as sound, but as a vibrating presence under her ribs. Evie continues:

> EVIE: Rest assured that Zork is at peace now. You needn't worry about him anymore. At least one of those bastards took the long way down.

> HEAPMONK: Thank you. You're good people for that.

> ROOTMUSE: o7, Zork.

> CTRLZ: Back to business? We've got a data dump to analyze.

HeapMonk drops off the thread briefly—Evie pictures him lighting a candle in the windowsill of whatever tax-dodge state he's in. There's a less frantic ping from him after. She takes it as a confirmation.

> EVIE: While I was out, did you get a hook on the secondary node?

> HEAPMONK: Yes. But you're not going to like the handshake. Mercer's net, for all we know, may very well be quantum-resistant. Seeded with time-variant hardware certs. We can't even replay our own packets.

> EVIE: And, if I just show up in person?

ROOTMUSE: Might as well bring a suicide note. Or a pie. Both will get eaten.

CTRLZ: What's your play, Cross? You go in hot and you'll be the one getting burned.

She stares at the cursor. The diner's TV is running weather, but nobody's paying attention. She types:

EVIE: I'm not going in hot. I just learned that the hard way.

She considers:

EVIE: We need another angle. I want evidence—data. Not just to take down monsters. I want to show the world what is real.

CTRLZ: Good. Finally thinking long game.

ROOTMUSE: We have one unused crack left. HeapMonk can take another pass at the staging server. But it's got a tripwire that will alert Vanta. You want to go all in, say the word.

Evie's hands move over the keyboard. There's a disconnect, like remote manipulation, but the pattern is all hers.

EVIE: Go all in.

HEAPMONK: Copy.

ROOTMUSE: You realize this will burn your last favors with us, right?

EVIE: After I'm done, there's nothing left to save.

There's a lull. On the TV, the forecast is for snow, then rain, then snow again. The retirees are shuffling pieces, one of them muttering about the decline of play in the computer age.

CtrlZ breaks the silence.

CTRLZ: Evie, you good?

She pauses. Looks around the diner. At the spoon in her coffee, the chip in the cup. The cheap, beige paint. The pale tension of her knuckles.

EVIE: I'm good. Just tired.

CTRLZ: That's when mistakes happen.

EVIE: Not this time.

She powers down the laptop and sits for a minute, not touching her sandwich, letting the caffeine and the adrenaline metabolize. The cold outside is nothing compared to the cold in her chest, but it's manageable.

Evie stomachs what she can to feed her body. Will need the energy tomorrow. After leaving a sizeable tip, she makes the long walk back to the motel. Door locked, gravity hauls her down to flump onto the bed. She grabs the remote and checks the news.

Haden's text is still there. She stares at it, thumb hovering.

Then... deletes.

Not because she's angry, but to avoid the obligation.

Evie logs into the backup comms, scans for any pings from HeapMonk or CtrlZ. There's nothing. Not yet. She glances at the time—nearly 1AM. Their main event is happening on a server farm somewhere, a digital war she can't even see.

She buries her face in the scarf, breathes it in, and waits for dawn.

Evie is up and out of bed before her body wants. The night sweated the adrenaline from her, but now her joints are locked and her mouth tastes like dry cleaning fluid. She gropes for her phone, snaps it on: 9:06 a.m.

The laptop boots instantly. She expects the usual deluge of pings and notifications, the chime of war room chatter, but the screen is quiet. The ETHOS channel is a string of missed messages, all from late last night:

> CTRLZ: At limit. No obvious entry vectors.

> HEAPMONK: We tried, Evie. It's not human.

> ROOTMUSE: They built Vanta to hunt us. It's not a firewall, it's a goddamn predator.

She scrolls up—registering all the failed attempts and escalating panic, then a gap, then the most recent:

> CTRLZ: We're calling it. Time to reassess.

She keys in, hands cold on the keys.

> EVIE: What? No luck on the fallback? How about something old-school?

No one replies. For a full minute, she stares at the blinking cursor, like it's a countdown clock for her own relevance. The motel's heat is still off, and the coffee machine grumbles like it resents being woken at this hour.

Another message pings:

> ROOTMUSE: What a sorry way to wake. Got nothing good. Had to walk the block, clear my head.

> EVIE: That bad?

> ROOTMUSE: Vanta is thorough. It closes every backdoor. We can't even bounce packets off the sensors.

> EVIE: What if I'm on-site?

> ROOTMUSE: It would know you were there before you cross the perimeter. The sensors are smarter now. Not just video—thermal, seismic, pressure. If they can't ID you, they'll isolate you, then expose you.

A pause, then:

> ROOTMUSE: Sorry. I'm not mincing words. I know you want the truth.

> EVIE: I want a way in.

ROOTMUSE: Hey.

ROOTMUSE: Evie is there.

CTRLZ: So?

ROOTMUSE: What if we introduce a physical exploit? We can seed you a payload, but you have to get it close to a server node. I'm thinking RFID. The ones outside are all fiber, no wireless. But I bet the gates have a chip reader.

EVIE: What's the risk?

HEAPMONK: Oh, certain death if they like. But not right away.

EVIE: Walk me through it.

ROOTMUSE: HeapMonk wrote a worm—smart, recursive, only works once. If you can flash it at the gatehouse, it will give us five, maybe ten minutes of control before Vanta recognizes and purges. You could be in the building by then.

EVIE: What about evidence? Can you reach his files then?

CTRLZ: No. What Root is leaving out is that's on you.

HEAPMONK: We rejected her plan because you're not a hacker.

ROOTMUSE: No. Evie is not a hacker. But maybe she could establish a remote node from within.

She closes the window, stares at the ceiling for a full minute. Her hands shake less than yesterday, but the dread is deep, running hot through her armpits and low in her gut. It isn't the dying part that bothers her; it's the possibility that she's the only one who can do this. They're talking about entering the lion's den and exposing herself for the greater threat to see. If she fails, June, Michael and everyone else will have been for nothing.

It was one thing to confront Mercer in a clinic, unannounced.

Her mind treads back over the spirit's progenitors—the fates they suffered. The Harbinger, and more importantly, herself, knows what happens to the exposed.

She runs a hand down her face, stands, and pulls her gear from the pack. Evie strips out of the old clothes, showers, and changes into a new base layer and jeans. Refreshed and ready, she finishes lacing her boots just as her phone buzzes. Another message.

CTRLZ: You're doing this, aren't you?

EVIE: Is there another play?

CTRLZ: Damn. Not that we can see.

EVIE: Then walk me through it. Step-by-step.

Chapter Nineteen

Connecting Dots

Morning comes with a gambit sure to pay off. Marcus Vaughn is weary of Detective Hayes' makeshift hotel war room. A waft of freshly brewed coffee barely tempered its taint of poly carpet. Marcus bounds in ahead of the others, throwing the door open with an energy reserved for men who haven't let go of the overnight adrenaline. Haden is already there, a silhouette against the window. He hasn't shaved, calculated to age him up in front of locals but not the Bureau. Marcus can appreciate that. Some days, you need to look like you're halfway in the grave.

This didn't need to be that.

He tosses the file folder onto the table and parks himself in a seat with a view of the entrance, while the others filter in. "I've got a theory," he says before Cass or Reyes can even start unpacking. "Wanna hear it?"

Haden doesn't flinch. "Go on."

Vaughn tries on a grin. "What if the Kansas City body was a message, but not for us? What if his own handler removed Volkov's heart? Follow me—Evie was tracking Volkov, shadowing him, which means anyone skilled enough to move product cross-border could spot her a mile off. If their chain of custody was about to be exposed, the only way to preserve it was to cut off the liability."

Cass clicks open her laptop, not looking at him, but he can see her lips move: "Jesus, Marcus."

Reyes just shrugs, eyebrow arched.

Marcus warms up his premise, letting it exude through his performance. "It's a clean kill, but it's also a message. The organ is gone, but the kill is theatrical, dramatic. That's how you make the threat stick: you do it big, public, and you leave just enough *weird* to stall law enforcement. Meanwhile, the handler is free, the shipment is dead in the water, and every snitch in the pipeline is too terrified to breathe."

For a second, no one interrupts. Haden just stares, half-lidded. He's not even writing it down.

Cass breaks first. "You're saying Evie was the trigger, not the weapon?"

He spreads his hands. "I'm saying she's being set up as a warning, not a killer."

Reyes adds, "That tracks with her MO. She's always been more observer than participant."

The room's tension eases by a single degree. It's working. He's buying Evie a possible out, the one commodity Marcus has to offer. Still, the performance needs to be airtight. "I mean, come on. You think she's going to slice a two-fifty Russian and haul the heart out herself? I know Cross. The gal is strategic, not blunt force."

Haden finally moves. He stands by the table, plants both hands on the lacquered wood, and pins Marcus with a look that belongs in a final interview room. "Then what would be your next move, Vaughn?"

"I'm saying there's a handler." Marcus cocks his head, lets the pause draw out. "If we find who wanted the message sent, we find our killer."

Haden nods, slow, but the lines at his temples deepen. There's something in the old man's eyes that Marcus can't quite name. "We can run with that. Reyes, check all points of entry from Canada down. I want the entire cross-border pipeline mapped. If there's a handler, there's a point of contact. Cass, look for weird traffic in Volkov's rental GPS. Anything that's a possible dead drop or meeting—flag it."

Reyes is already on her laptop, fingers a blur. Cass mutters something about "dark web tradecraft" but is doing her own kind of magic. Marcus leans back, lets himself feel the buzz of the room. For the first time in a while, he's working a case that doesn't involve rubber-stamping profiles for bored field agents. There's a puzzle here, a real one. One he's got his mitts on.

Haden adds, "And someone track Cross. If she's still anywhere near Missouri, I want eyes."

The room falls into a productive hush: only the tap of keys and the occasional flip of a page. Marcus thumbs through his own files, but his actual work is inward—counting the steps between Evie and the truth. He already knows there's a link between this kill and the Cartographer, but he'll be damned if he's going to put it in the open. Haden's seen his file. They both know what Marcus did, and didn't do, five years ago. There's nothing to say that hasn't already scorched him.

Now is his time to rise from the ashes.

His mind runs over the old tape: Evie, hollowed out after June vanished, propping herself up with cases until she broke the rules for a higher good. He respected that. He even envied it.

Yet, Marcus is still thinking it over when Reyes sits up, eyes narrow. "Got a ping."

Cass swivels in. "Evie?"

Reyes winces. "Pretty sure. Her old credentials flagged an admin login in Jackson Hole. Three hours ago. It's a passive hit. She may not even know the connection is semi-active."

Marcus tries not to react, but there's a pinch at the base of his spine. "What's in Jackson Hole?"

"Besides choice skiing? Not much." Reyes flips the screen so Cass can see. "But get this: she's downloaded two sets of satellite images. Both of them are remote facilities. One is a private medical center up near Mt. Saint John; the other—" Reyes frowns, turns the laptop so the others can see, "—is a private airstrip. Both within driving distance of each other."

Cass leans in. "Coordinates?"

"Here." Reyes double-taps the screen.

Haden pushes off the table. "Good catch, Reyes. Let's book a flight out to Wyoming. We can pack it in here. I want boots on the ground ASAP."

Marcus stands, stretching out the kinks in his back. "You got it."

There's a flicker of something on Haden's face—guilt? But then it's gone, and he's all business again, barking orders, setting up a conference call with Quantico. Grabbing his jacket, Marcus follows Reyes to the hall.

Outside, the corridor is empty, the early-morning quiet broken only by the hum of vending machines and the TV in the breakfast nook.

Reyes slows down, glances back at him. "Why'd you sell that theory so hard?"

He doesn't miss a step. "Because it's the right one."

She snorts. "Uh-huh. Right."

He shrugs. "She's one of us."

"Is she? Is she really?"

Marcus leans closer, lowers his voice. "Don't you want to believe there's at least one person out there who still gives a damn about the why?"

She looks away, then back at him. "I used to."

Reyes departs with her deliberate cat-foot stride, leaving Marcus at the edge of a breakfast nook. He digs in the pockets of his mind for one more good move. Anything that will help cement his narrative. In the end, he thumbs at his phone, pretending to review notes.

He's done well. But they're closing in, all the same.

Back down the hall, their local detective pushes out of the conference room. He walks two steps as if on autopilot, then slows and hangs a left down a side corridor. Not toward the front desk, but deeper into the hotel. Something in the set of Hayes' shoulders and the soft, off-beat way he hesitates rings as somewhat apart from the others.

How is the Detective taking this turn of events? His services are no longer required?

Waiting a beat, Marcus trails off after him.

He rounds a corner and catches himself before he's spotted. Hayes has stopped with his cell to his ear. Marcus creeps back out of sight, listening. While he can't pick up the other end of the conversation, the Detective's side conveys plenty.

"We'll need a layover to refuel, but I *can* get ahead of this. You want the collar; this is how—" A hesitation, then Hayes again. "Don't log it in the system until we've cleared with the DA. This is more than a bit outside our jurisdiction."

Wait.

What the hell is Hayes diverting?

Chapter Twenty

She has a Plan

E vie pilots the Fiesta up the last quarter-mile of mountain switchback with her body rigid against the seatback. The frost has not lifted, but daylight pretends it could. Her dashboard clock lies by an hour, still set to central standard.

She has replayed the scenario a hundred times, but each pass ends in a different failure: digital, social, or simply existential. The rules of engagement here are opaque, and every approach to the compound feels like a variant on suicide, some faster than others.

Of course, none of them accounts for her rider.

Evie has no way to factor that.

Her hands, gloved under thrift-store wool, grip the wheel at ten and two. The RFID card rides in the console cup, already slotted to the black square of the device HeapMonk recommended. The laptop in the passenger seat hums a faint, sub-audible pulse, wireless adapters live and hunting.

She will do this by the numbers. Swipe the card. The worm will auto-trigger gate access while Vanta is distracted by the worm. Deliver her flowers to the home and scope out any computers. All she needs is one USB port. Pop in the exploit dongle and exit the property. Ethos will do the rest. Still, so much is left up to chance.

Above, the mountain crest splits the sky into two: one side blue so sharp it feels like a threat, the other a drift of overexposed white.

She has time for one last check. Evie pulls the car over at a turnout a few hundred yards shy of the compound. Here, the shoulder is packed snow. The air, as she steps out, is punishing—so dry it crackles in the throat. She opens the back hatch and begins the sequence:

- Pop the hood. Unclip the old floral delivery magnet, slap it onto the door.

- Open the floral toolkit, fake a few dings and smudges onto her hands and coat. Not too much. They're expecting a driver, not a demolitionist.

- Uncoil the phone charger and check the wireless connection. The battery is at 94%. Every bit helps.

She snaps the trunk shut and stands for a moment, letting her breath fog. The edge of the compound looms up ahead—a mass of glass, steel, and dark stone, perched at the knife-edge of a ravine. There is no pretense of belonging here, no effort at camouflage. Satellite images show what to expect. The driveway up is single-lane, guarded by a half-circle of carbon-reinforced posts and a gunmetal gate that looks borrowed from a transhuman movie set. The call box awaits.

She slides back into the car, knuckles tightening against the steering wheel. Exhale. It's just another cold call, she tells herself.

Her Fiesta's heater is a joke, but she cranks it up anyway.

The drive to the gate is thirty seconds of rehearsed calm. She parks about ten feet from the threshold, careful to line the florist logo to the camera's angle. There are no signs, no security vehicles—only a camera dome set on a stalk, and a discreet, embossed plaque that reads, in three languages, PRIVATE RESIDENCE.

Evie leans over the passenger seat, pretending to fuss with the bouquet box—with three crisp lilies and a garish bow. The idea is to look bored, maybe a little hungover, just another blue-collar courier running behind.

She waits.

The camera rotates, clicks once. In her jacket, the phone vibrates: RootMuse's exploit is live, pinging the gate's access panel. All Evie has to do is present the card, and the virus will handshake in, root through the security stack, and open up a brief corridor for HeapMonk's attack package. Five minutes, maybe less, before it is discovered and purged.

She breathes. "Showtime."

Pushing open the car door, Evie steps out into the cold. The gate is a good five yards away, but she walks slow—casual, not sneaky. She palms the RFID card, carrying it and the bouquet together.

At two paces from the reader, there is a beep. She stops to look up. A camera LED lights up.

She parts her lips to speak, "Hel—"

"Mrs. Cross," a deep voice says. "What an unexpected surprise."

It's not what she expects. This isn't a rent-a-cop, or a post-Soviet bruiser with a tactical lisp. Instead, it is crisp, cultivated, and almost amused. Male, early forties, with the kind of diction that suggests careful thought.

Oh gawd. That's not the worst part. *They know it's me.*

Evie's mind lurches. Not just because they know, but because the voice is also wrong. It doesn't match any of her models for what she'd expect from Mercer's people. She runs a linguistics loop in her head: most likely, it's a synthetic—some AI-enabled concierge, patched together for this one, precise location.

She swallows hard.

The speaker continues, "I believe there has been a terrible misunderstanding between yourself and other involved parties. It is one, that dare I say, could be construed as completely reprehensible. Thankfully, your presence notes an opportunity for all parties to come to an understanding."

Evie glares, incredulous. "Uh..."

How does one even respond?

"Thank you for coming all this way," the voice continues. "We would be delighted to clarify matters for you in person."

Evie's stomach flips, but she manages a nod, playing along.

"Of course," the voice is honeyed, pleased. "You may enter. Proceed to the main entrance."

With that, there's a buzz. Iron gates fold inward with a deliberate grace, each bar glinting daylight as they interlock back in on themselves. Their framework transforms what had been a barrier into a high-tech threshold, as though the estate itself bowed to receive a guest.

A chill runs down the length of her spine. It's not just the AI. It's the way it says, 'You may enter'—as if to imply she is being allowed, not because she fooled anyone, but because she's already been processed and found *trivial.*

Evie stands there, twitching glances back to her car.

Nowhere to run. She could hop in her car and hightail it back down the mountain. But if she bails, she's lost the one shot at getting RootMuse's exploit in place. If she proceeds... Well, she's obviously walking into a trap.

Shoulders slumping, Evie eyes the flowers.

Not much point in pretenses now. Walking back to the Fiesta, she pops the trunk, and stows her faux delivery. Breathing out through her nose, Evie slams the trunk. Then strolls back to the driver's seat and climbs in.

She doesn't put it in gear right away.

Instead, she considers.

They always underestimate. They do it with a smile or an algorithm, but it always comes down to the same calculus: small woman, damaged, brittle as a matchstick. It's exactly how those two special forces goons Mercer hired to 'clean up' his mess had lost to her. And it'll be how she brings his empire down now.

Evie palms the card and presses it into her jacket. She gives herself three breaths to regret her life choices, then throws the car in gear, rolling slowly through the gap in the gates. The world on the other side is scrubbed and geometric, every hedge and flagstone obviously designed by someone who liked nature but loved the control of it even better. The driveway snakes past a bronze sculpture—an abstraction of a neural network, each node rendered as an eye, the whole thing red-rusted and gleaming in the sun.

Ahead, the glass-and-stone mansion dominates the horizon, a hive for the future, setting itself above the world. At the top of the steps, the double doors slide open, and a woman steps out onto the landing.

She's tall, sleek, and clad head-to-toe in navy blue—blazer, slacks, even the turtleneck. Evie catalogues the stance: not armed, but arms loose and relaxed. Her hair is silver, cropped close but not severe, and the face carries a subdued smile—more pronounced in the eyes than the mouth. She radiates the comfort of someone who's been in far worse standoffs than this.

Evie pulls up, pops it in park, leaves the keys, and climbs out. She walks slowly, taking in the security cameras at every corner, the silent, panoramic sweep of Vanta's presence.

"Mrs. Cross," the woman calls. Her accent might be Swiss or Dutch, the vowels sanded down to near nothing. "Welcome."

Chapter
Twenty-One

Partner Up

Hayes coordinates the state chopper himself. He checks his pack twice: sidearm, notepad, bottled water. Then he walks the tarmac in the late morning cold, the east wind rattling the hangar doors at Kansas City's smaller municipal strip. The chopper—slicked in blue with a brash white MO STATE POLICE painted up the tail—crouches on its wheels, humming and ready.

Deputy McBride is already there, helmet tucked underarm. He offers Hayes the same raised eyebrow as the last time, the one that says: are you sure you want to be doing this? Hayes affirms with a silent nod.

He climbs in, keeping his coat zipped to the jawline. McBride buckles in and flicks a couple of switches. "Backseat clear, Detective?"

Hayes looks. There are a couple of empty seats.

"Just us," he says, voice flat.

They're about to roll when a lean figure runs up the tarmac, collar popped, a windbreaker flapping around his hips. Hayes recognizes his clean-shaven dome—too upright, too eager: Vaughn.

Marcus pops open the hatch without waiting for an invitation. "Couldn't let you get all the glory, eh Detective Hayes?"

Hayes grunts. "Just... What do you think you're doing?"

Marcus swings in, squeezing his knees between the front seats. "Caught wind you might need some backup. Haden thought you could use a chaperone. Lucky me!"

McBride, eyes on the fuel meter, snorts. "The more, the merrier, gentlemen. If you're all ready to play nice, we can get moving."

The chopper kicks off the ground, skidding a little on the crosswind, then climbs in a slow, deliberate arc. Kansas City drops away, shrinking to gray polygons and car ant-lines, which then dissolve behind the clouds.

For five minutes, neither man speaks. Then Marcus, unable to stay quiet, pipes up: "You know, I volunteered. Any guesses why?"

Liam shakes his head, watching the terrain scroll beneath them.

"It's not about the case," Marcus says. "Well, it is. But not like what's in the paperwork."

Liam remains quiet.

"Evie saved my bacon. Literally," Marcus says. "Well, not literally about bacon, more about my life. If she's out there, she deserves to know someone's coming who doesn't think she's a monster."

Hayes looks over his shoulder. "Is that why you're redirecting the Bureau off her?"

Marcus smirks. "She's a mess, but she's one of ours."

Hayes digests this. It's not the answer he'd expected, but it makes sense. He wonders if Marcus ever really saw Evie, or if he's projecting some old loyalty onto her. Maybe it doesn't matter.

"So," Marcus says, "What's your angle?"

"Simple," Hayes says. "My superiors want the collar. When it comes down to it, I'll be the one to bring her in."

Marcus nods. "Or put her down?"

Hayes doesn't answer.

The world outside the window is white and blue, splayed with irrigation lines and frost-bitten fields. Somewhere ahead, the Teton Mountains await, and the woman who might be a suspect, a witness, or a victim.

Hayes focuses on the engine drone numb his ears. He wants to be ready when the moment comes.

At twelve thousand feet, Nebraska is an infinite sheet of sun-bleached nothing, broken only by the desperate geometry of crops and the occasional thread of interstate. Hayes studies the ground even though he knows the map by heart; it's the habit of a man who needs land under his boots.

Once again, Marcus is the first to nudge at the silence. Leaning forward, he taps at Liam. "You ever get used to this part?"

"Which part?" Hayes knows the answer but wants to make Vaughn spell it out.

"The wait. The interim. The part where you don't know if you're chasing the devil or just another sad sack with a midlife crisis."

Hayes sips from his coffee thermos. "Is that how you see it?"

"I'm just projecting from an outsider looking in." Marcus grins, teeth white and predatory. "Curious how you think we feds handle such things."

Hayes glances at the pilot, then at Marcus. "You closed the Cartographer case, didn't you?"

"Yeah." Marcus's smile holds, but it's less joy than showing teeth. "You ever wonder if the brass cares more about the story than the truth?"

Hayes considers. "I am sure they do."

"A guy like me," Marcus says, "I'm not cut out for truth. I'm malleable. You?" He looks at Hayes sideways. "You're more of a math guy, aren't you? Add it up, make every number fit, or it bugs you."

It's a weird thing, feeling seen and also measured for depth. Hayes hates that Marcus is right, not just about him, but about the whole damn system. "You always profile your ride-alongs?"

"I profile everything," Marcus says. "You're stubborn, but you're not a cowboy. So what's the play?"

Hayes shrugs. "The play is we get there before anyone else. We see what there is to see. We make sure nobody buries what's inconvenient." How many times has he watched cases get rewritten in memos—how many times he's looked at the facts and seen the outline of a shoe print, only to have it scuffed away by the next morning?

"I lied," Marcus says, fingers toying with the zipper on his jacket. "It's not that I don't care about the truth. I just care more about how it's subjected to the people who get steamrolled by it."

He means Evie. Hayes shrugs again, less defensive this time. "She's lucky to have you in her corner."

Marcus shakes his head. "She's never needed me. Evie only ever needs the next question, the next thing to chase." He's earnest for a moment, less peacock, more man. "What about you, Hayes? Why do you care?"

Hayes watches the steam rise from his coffee. "Who said I do?"

"You wouldn't have run this chopper out of your own jurisdiction if you didn't. Missouri breeds some impressive bureaucrats, but I doubt you're one of them."

The compliment permeates the space between them, and Liam lets it hang. He turns the question over, finding no neat answer. "Maybe I'm just tired of watching the wrong people win." Marcus laughs. "That's it, then. You're a real romantic."

"That better not show up in any reports." Hayes seals the cover on his thermos. The only certainty was that once this reached Quantico, no one would remember who gave a damn. The Bureau grinds up its stories and serves them cold. He checks his phone. Mercifully, no calls from Haden, only a half-dozen stale notifications. For now, they are off-leash.

Hayes runs through the evidence in his head: the murdered courier, the harvested heart, the trail of rentals, the way Evie initially kept popping up like a splinter nobody could extract. He builds a model of her mind, step by logical step, and tries to anticipate her next move.

"She's not running," he says, more to himself than Marcus.

"No," Marcus agrees. "This is a hunt. Question is, is she prey or predator?"

Hayes looks at him. "You came up with that as a profiler?"

"From the look in her eyes," Marcus says. "People only get that look when they're on a mission. Not to escape. To finish. I'm just not sure she knows if she's being played or not. She might consider herself a wolf and not notice the polar bear coming up from behind. Take it from me, it's happened before."

Hayes accepts that.

The world outside grows rougher, the grid lines giving way to abrupt cliffs and rivers, the land rising under them. He checks the GPS, then the altimeter.

When they cross into Wyoming, Marcus sits forward. "You got a plan?"

Hayes does. "You're going to talk. I'll listen."

Marcus laughs, loud enough for McBride to glance back, then shrugs. "Fine by me. I like the sound of my own voice."

Chapter Twenty-Two

Cordial Invitations

There's a protocol for entering another predator's den; Evie is uncertain which script applies here. Hostage negotiation? Arrest warrant? Suicide mission? She does have a good guess which this is. But never like this—never when the target's weaponized the house itself, when the security system pronounces your name with the purr of a cat crouching before the pounce.

She stands beside her Ford Fiesta, some thirty yards off the main portico. The wind at this altitude is less a breeze and more a series of precision strikes—sharp, direct, intent on finding any exposed flesh. She knots June's scarf tight to the hollow of her throat. Her hands, checking for the inner pocket, the RFID card & USB stick. She leaves her gun in the car. There wouldn't be much of a point in it. They'd just take it from her, anyway.

Above, the sky domes blue and infinite, but everything below the roofline belongs to Vanta now. A camera sights every hedge and path, every molecule of air sniffed and analyzed by the system. The house itself is not the only creature here with less mercy than Evie.

She takes the steps, pulse at a baseline hum. No doubt, the AI has already processed her. It will have run her face through a thousand permutations—databases, social media. The only surprise is that she's allowed past the gates.

The silver-tressed woman just stands waiting at the stair top. The effect is mathematical: she doesn't occupy space so much as define it. Her navy suit is crisp, and the lines of her body—slim, efficient, the shape of a blade. Her face is neither welcoming nor hostile; it's the quiet of a gun left on a kitchen table.

"Mrs. Cross," she says. *Not 'Special Agent.' Not 'Evelyn.'* Her voice is a coolant, precise in its dispensation. "I am Irina Kovács, Mr. Mercer's PA. As a profiler, you'll appreciate how outside our parameters your appearance is today."

"Surprise traffic on the mountain," Evie says, deadpan. She steps inside, noting the floor: black marble, but inlaid with thin lines of gold and iridescent blue—like the veins in some impossible mineral. The room's warmth registers after a beat, gentle but absolute. In a single step, she's gone from windburned to encased in the temperature of someone else's comfort zone.

Irina closes the door. No click, no sound, but Evie feels the vibration run up her legs.

"I have to say," Irina begins, "we also anticipated a less... personal approach. A phone call, perhaps, or an encrypted message to Mercer's legal."

Evie shrugs. "If I thought your firewalls could be breached, I'd have stayed in my pajamas."

"Of course." Irina's smile is formal.

The air hangs with something sour—a faint chemical note that undercuts the rich, clean aromas of polish and money. Behind Irina, the foyer widens into a cathedral of glass and art: a Kiefer canvas, a pair of Brancusi knockoffs, a freestanding wall laser-etched with what looks like neural mapping, though the lines converge to spell out words she can't parse at this angle. The security cameras aren't just visible; they're displayed, as if to say, 'This is what matters here.'

"May I take your coat?" Irina says, not waiting for a reply before gliding behind Evie. Her hands alight across her midsection in a subtle frisk, before sliding it off at her shoulders. Even through the fabric, Evie senses the absence of heat: Irina is cold, in every register.

Evie lets the coat slip off, but refuses to unloop June's scarf.

Irina doesn't comment. She folds the coat with the grace of a hotelier, but there's a martial edge to her every movement.

"This way, please," she says, and pivots.

Evie follows, cataloging: There are three exits from the foyer, but only one looks unsecured—a hallway lined with photos, large-format black-and-whites. Few of them are of people. Instead, they're satellite shots, arrays of brain matter, the whorl of an iris, a fiber-optic cable in cross-section. Each image is a portrait, but the subject is data.

Irina walks at a measured pace, neither rushing nor dragging. Evie falls into step exactly one pace behind—close enough to see the contour of Irina's ears, which are perfect, unadorned, a little too still. If Irina's packing a weapon, it's not obvious, but she's got the gait of someone who expects violence and has already rehearsed the choreography.

"Would you like tea?" Irina asks, gesturing at a seat.

Evie takes the chair, angles it so her back isn't to the corridor.

Irina catches this. "Being prudent. Yes."

Evie wonders what the woman's file says. People like this always have files, dossiers within corporate structures. Childhood in a post-Soviet East, maybe, or an upbringing somewhere Baltic, with enough raw intelligence to land a retainer for one of the world's most dangerous technocrats.

Tea arrives on a cart, brought by someone Evie refuses to dignify with the word 'butler.' His build is too solid, special ops probably, but she'd guess not quite tier one, his stance and hair cropped tight. The man pours with ritual exactness.

"Milk? Sugar?" Irina asks.

"Black," says Evie, not breaking eye contact.

A long moment passes, and then the 'butler' leaves. The door at the far end hisses shut.

"You have questions," Irina says.

"Where's Mercer." Evie asks, not as a question.

Irina gives the smallest of shrugs, as if conceding a point in chess. "He's upstairs. When it suits him, he'll see you."

Evie sips her tea. It's perfect, so hot it scalds her tongue.

Irina tips her head. "Do you know why you're really here, Mrs. Cross?"

"I know why I came."

A flicker, not of emotion, but of calculation. "You want to believe this is about the Cartographer, or the transplant chain, or about vengeance for your daughter. But you are mistaken."

Evie feels the Harbinger twitch, just beneath the surface of her skin, an itch at her vertebrae. The entity wants to break this woman's composure—for whatever is underneath.

"I have information you need," Evie says, voice flattening into ice. "But I'm not giving it to you until—"

"Please." Irina holds up a hand. "There is no leverage here. Not for either of us. I am simply... facilitating."

Evie leans forward. "I'm not here for a performance review."

Irina's smile finally becomes real, and it's worse than the alternative. "Of course not. But you see, Mrs. Cross, there are elements in play here that are out of your control. Mr. Mercer is—how do you say?—in mourning. And when a man like that mourns, the world can be at risk of getting buried with him."

A pulse of anxiety threads through Evie's chest, but she refuses to show it.

The Harbinger claws at the inside of her sternum. Every profiler bone in her body says this is where the game shifts, where the prey realizes the cage is not the real prison.

Irina stands, signals for Evie to follow. "It's time."

They ascend the stairs, past a series of doors that Evie notes as numbered, not named. The interior is even more clinical up here, with the walls becoming glass and the carpet so dense it absorbs sound. Evie counts the security sensors, the pattern of the cameras. If things go bad, she'll have to make a break for it at the landing and use the statue as a shield. There are no weapons within reach, but a pen through the eye works just as well as a bullet, if you have the nerve.

Irina stops before a door at the end of the hall. She swipes an ID badge against the sensor, and the door slides open with an intake of air.

Inside is a room like no other. It's both a sanctuary and a medical theater: the lights are dim and indirect, the view out onto the valley so wide it feels like they're floating in the sky. At the center is a hospital bed, but so disguised in layers of silk and tech that it seems at once sacred and monstrous. The only sounds in the room are the hiss of oxygen and the subtle, metronomic blip of a pulse monitor and EEG machine.

Standing beside is what's left of Alexander Mercer.

He does not look up.

Evie has certainly seen plenty of his photos, but in person he's less a human and more a hollow scaffolding of human will. His hair is white, his face tanned and tight, the eyes blue—flat as lake ice. He's built like someone who's fought hard to keep the world at bay, and the suit he wears is so understated it's barely acknowledged as clothing.

Irina stands back, closing the door. She seems almost deferential.

Mercer speaks without looking at her. "Who is this?"

Irina clears her throat. "Mr. Mercer, this is Mrs. Evelyn Cross. She's the FBI agent who actually solved the old Cartographer case. I'm afraid she may have played a role in our previous delivery." She says it the way some people announce a Nobel laureate, with an edge of professional respect.

Mercer turns, his gaze pinning Evie like a thumbtack to the moment. His mouth is a line, not smiling, not angry—just registering.

"My daughter is dying." His words hang.

Evie looks to the bed, sees the outline of a young woman, barely twenty, unconscious or worse. The tubes and wires running from her body pulse with faint light. The monitors a gentle beep, all its telemetry rerouted to a bank of screens at the far wall.

"Celeste," he says the name like a prayer. "She has H.A.P. Heredi-tary Amyloid Polyneuropathy. It's a rare disorder, almost always fatal. You inherit a broken gene, and your body builds up the wrong pro-tein—amyloid—until the nerves and organs stop working. Sometimes it's the heart first; other times, the liver. For Celeste, it's a cascade of several."

Evie stands there, hands in fists.

"Five years ago," Mercer goes on, "she was thriving. College. Skiing. The works. Then she started fainting. Next, she couldn't walk a block without pain. Later, she couldn't… remember." He glances at the monitors, and for a second she thinks he might cry. He doesn't. "We did everything. The Cartographer had a plan. When that fell through, all we were left with were clinical trials. Off-label infusions. Then those failed. You see, it's a time bomb. And you can't defuse it with money, influence, or cleverness. Only organs." He looks up. "She's not in a coma because she's dying. She's in a coma because we can't let her wake up for one more failed surgery. Or one more explanation of why her legs don't work, or why her voice shakes, or why her father—who promised her everything—can't deliver." Mercer closes his eyes. The only movement is in his right hand, which rests on Celeste's. The daughter's hand is birdlike, thin as a glove, fingers splayed across the sheets.

He breathes in, the effort audible.

Evie's hands clench around the scarf. The Harbinger is up in her larynx now, pressing on her voice. She wants to say something, any-thing, but finds nothing.

Mercer finally looks at her.

Really looks.

"If it were your daughter, Mrs. Cross," he says, "how far would you go?"

Chapter Twenty-Three

Open Books

Refueling at Cheyenne Regional is but one of their limitations, but needed to get ahead of Haden's team. The chopper sets down behind the firehouse, where the refueling crew acts like they're running a Formula One pit stop. McBride hops out to stretch and shake hands with the fuel guy, leaving Hayes and Marcus alone in the back. The rotors tick down, and Hayes uses the lull to have his turn at questioning.

Marcus has shed his Bureau windbreaker, exposing a shirt that looks department-issue but fits like something from a thrift shop. He's popped the top off a Red Bull—either his third or his fourth, Hayes has lost count.

"So, Marcus. I understand you collared the Cartographer a while back. What's the real story? You know, between two detectives." Liam delivers it flat, expecting Marcus to parry or at least posture.

Instead, the profiler keeps his eyes on the tarmac, spinning the can, then finally shrugs.

"Outside the basics?" Marcus says. "Real guy's a serial neurosurgeon, carves away brains like a topographical map. Ran a clinic for rich weirdos."

Liam allows the silence to probe.

The Red Bull spins.

"The details aren't that interesting," Marcus goes on. "Except for one. We got a search warrant for a Dr. Shepherd's offices, you know, after we connected the dots. Haden's team was supposed to go in, catalog everything, standard Bureau stuff. Except Shepherd is one of those freaks who anticipates law enforcement like a chess move."

He glances at Hayes now, a little smirk like he's waiting for a punchline. "We went through his records, the storage, his personal office... Nothing. Not a single connection, not a fingerprint. Everything immaculate. You could have done a full forensic sweep and not found even a tax dodge."

Hayes nods, letting Marcus pace the story.

Marcus's voice drops. "Then there was this tremor. Tiny, but enough to rattle glassware off a shelf. Reyes sees a hairline crack behind a bookshelf. Next thing, we're swinging open a hidden compartment, and there's this safe, bolted to the studs. We get it open. Inside there's a stack of notebooks."

He's warming up now. Marcus Vaughn is the kind of guy who only really comes alive when he's at the center of a story. Hayes lets him run.

"They're not just medical logs. These are... Let's call them journals. Manifestos. Maps, drawings, diagrams of every victim, and enough self-incriminating detail to make Shepherd a three-time loser in the courts. We bag them up, chain of custody the whole way. The next morning, the judge throws it out. Says there was a break-in the night before. Claims it was a plant, a setup. Who knows, maybe even a prank."

Hayes's brows hitch. "You're kidding me."

"Wish I were," Marcus says. "The judge might have been a family friend of Shepherd's lawyer, for all I know. Instant conflict of interest, they said. The whole thing vanished in a fog of process."

Hayes takes this in. "What about the chain of custody? You have the evidence."

Marcus shrugs. "Didn't matter. Once the journals were tainted, everything else got reclassified as circumstantial. And you know what happens to circumstantial." He spins the Red Bull again, not drinking. "Shepherd couldn't even be arrested. Two days later, IA's office crawled up into our department. We got reassigned."

Hayes runs a hand over his jaw. "How did that sit with Evie?"

This time, Marcus laughs, the sound as dry as old paper. "She blamed herself. Said if she'd found a different angle—gone digital, or leveraged the data faster—it might've stuck. But that's not the actual story."

Hayes waits.

"The real story," Marcus says, "my guess is our Supervisory Special Agent Haden needed a scapegoat. Shepherd was too high-profile to fail. But Cross? She was perfect. Recent trauma, too smart for her own good, always poking at the wrong enemies. Unofficially, they painted her as a rogue operator. Said she pushed too hard, risked the case for glory. Haden appeared to protect her, but it was over before he got his brief settled. I figure, someone had to take the hit."

Hayes holds up a hand. "Wait. Are you telling me the Bureau burned its own profiler for optics?"

Marcus's eyes spark, maybe the only genuine emotion he's shown all morning. "You worked in the military, right? You know the drill. When command needs a fall guy, they pick the one who won't fight back. Or the one who's already lost too much to care."

"Evie was a fall guy."

"She was the only one who wanted ownership of the thing," Marcus says. "After her daughter, after the Cartographer, she just let it happen. Didn't file an appeal. Never went to the press. Just drifted off, hoping it will erase whatever guilt she carries."

Hayes is silent for a moment, watching the clouds boil over the hillsides. "So what do you think? She's out here to finish what she started, or to punish herself?"

Marcus smiles, but it's more a wound than a gesture. "I think people like Evie don't know the difference. When you've been punished for a crime, some part of you figures you might as well commit it. Even if you didn't. And after a while, you get tempted—just to see if it feels any different when it's real."

Hayes's pulse flares at the admission. "Is that what you think she's doing? Making it real?"

"Her appearance flagged the courier's death. She left the clues just barely in sight. You ever wonder if she wanted us to follow her?"

Hayes lets out a breath. "You're the profiler, Vaughn. I'm just a cop."

"No, you're not," Marcus says. "You don't chase a case across state lines just for the collar."

Hayes changes tack. "Alright, then. What aren't you telling me?"

Marcus barks a laugh, short and surgical. "See, I knew you were more than a badge. There is one thing I didn't say. Not to Haden, not to the Bureau."

He leans forward—the Red Bull can forgotten in his lap.

"Evie shared a theory. A pet theory. She believed Shepherd was a front."

Hayes's mind races. "A front for what?"

"Not what—who." Marcus's eyes lock with Hayes'. "She thought Shepherd was working for someone bigger. Someone with the means to cover up the entire operation, to buy the judge, the DA, even the Bureau's silence."

Hayes's tongue dries. "And that would be?"

"Billionaire… Alexander… Mercer." Marcus flumps back in his seat.

Liam cocks him a look.

A slow nod. "She had a file. Traced the black-market medical gear, the funding, all the way through several shell companies. But couldn't connect the dots. Never got proof."

For a second, the world outside the chopper is just whiteout, a fog of revelation and nothing else. Hayes says, "Did you tell Haden?"

"No." Marcus looks away. "I wanted to, but… It's one thing to have your career kicked in the nuts. Another to put a bullet through it. If the Bureau thought Haden was after Mercer, they'd stick him in Alaska. And if it turned out Evie was wrong… Woof! That'd be the end of it."

Hayes turns this over. "So what now?"

Marcus frowns. "You're the first person I've told. If she's going after Mercer, it means she's got nothing left to lose. And if she's got nothing left to lose, then there's no telling how far this goes."

He looks at the refueling crew, now buttoning up the tanks and running a check on the rotors. Hayes sees the moment: a set of choices lining up in a row, each more dangerous than the last.

Holding over Marcus for another long beat, he says, "However this pans out, you have to tell Haden. Bring him in. You don't want this to come from me."

Marcus nods, resigned. "That's fair."

McBride returns, helmet dangling from one hand, face pinked by the wind. "All set, Detectives. ETA to Jackson Hole is two and a half hours, longer if the wind holds."

Hayes nods, then turns to the pilot. "I've got a slight change in our destination."

McBride's eyebrows rise. "Orders?"

"We're heading straight for Mercer's airfield residence," Hayes says. "Get us there first. The medical facility can wait."

There's a long pause as McBride looks from Hayes to Marcus, as if seeking confirmation or a mutiny. Marcus just closes his eyes and leans back.

The chopper lifts, slicing through the air. The world below blurs, roads and rivers and boundaries gone. All that remains is the thing at the center of it, the cold and the question.

Hayes ponders Evie: that night relaxing with a beer, hair backlit by the porch heater, fingers twitching as if in muscle memory. He thinks of Alexei's body on the slab, heart scooped clean, and wonders how much of the story was even left to be written.

He glances at Marcus. The profiler is staring at the horizon, lost in his own algorithms.

For once, there's a sense that he's ahead of the case. Not by much, but maybe just enough.

Liam sets his jaw. "Let's do this."

Chapter Twenty-Four

Moral Power

The room is still, glass and lacquer, all hospital chic, with silk draping the IV tree and a set of monitors so flat they might as well be paintings. Mercer's emaciated daughter lies under a stack of expensive linens.

He waits. The line of his jaw, the flatness in his voice. Mercer is giving her the space to process, but also clarifying that she is, in this moment, on his clock.

"Mrs. Cross... how far would you go?"

Evie stands stock-still at the bedside, her breath seething through her nostrils.

The question slides under her ribs and splits there, forked. Her answer is already known, has been since the moment she found the dark splash on June's comforter and the absence everywhere else. She would burn the world for her daughter, and if she were not strong enough, she'd engineer a blaze to do the rest.

The Harbinger flexes. A skritch at the base of her skull, a rush in her blood that wants to obliterate every other person in the room. But that's just the trauma. It's what she's here to fight.

She takes Celeste in. The face is round, jaw squared by muscle loss, lips blue at the seam. There's a patch of hair at the left temple that someone's brushed, in the way you do when you want the patient to look nice. Maybe he pays someone to love his daughter on his behalf, or maybe he's so used to the power of money that he assumes feeling is just a product you purchase in bulk.

This is all just too damn much.

"I see what you're doing," Evie says. "Do you honestly believe I'm going to empathize with you?"

Mercer shrugs, his movement economical. "Understanding is all."

"Don't," Evie says. Her tongue is sanded raw, the metallic aftertaste of a panic attack coming on. "Don't put this on me."

He looks at her, and his eyes are not cruel. They're old, and flat, and just so tired.

Irina watches from the wall. Not looming, not gloating. Just a presence, a blade laid on the windowsill.

Evie clears her throat. "You're right. I would do anything for my daughter." She points at Celeste with her chin. "Even if it meant dealing with devils." Her voice cracks. "That's how we ended up here."

She wants to throttle him. Evie wants to pull the plug on the monitor, break the glass, shatter the illusion of his perfectly insulated grief. Instead, she lets the words pile up in her chest, then pushes them out, one at a time.

"You know what your money does, Mr. Mercer? It doesn't make you less desperate. It just spreads the collateral damage farther. Do you really want to know what you and I have in common?"

He lifts his chin.

"We're both guilty," she says. "But at least I'm willing to own it."

The Harbinger snaps at the leash, but she smothers it. Not now.

Mercer says nothing.

Evie steps closer, lowering her voice. "I've spent the last five years living with the idea that if I had just found a way—one more angle, one more question—maybe June would be alive. Maybe she could be comatose instead in a fancy suite, but at least she'd be breathing. You know what I did when I ran out of angles? I built one. I broke every protocol, every law, every scrap of morality I had left, just to try to make the universe less random."

Mercer's eyelids flicker. He is listening. Not like a mark, not like a cop, but like a man who knows the cost of belief.

"You want a deal?" she says. "Here it is: you confess. You tell the FBI everything about your operation. You give up your fixers, your doctors, your blood money, and—" she swallows, "and you give me everything you know about my daughter. Do that, and I'll not only turn you in... I'll even turn myself in. We can both rot."

Irina's smile is a paper cut. "My, my."

Evie ignores her. She's locked on Mercer, waiting for the reaction, the scramble, the denial.

Instead, he just frowns. "What does *your* daughter have to do with any of this?"

"What?" Her world tips. Evie blinks. "What do you mean..."

Evie is certain for one boiling second that this is some performance, an ultra-rich sociopath's gaslight. But it isn't. Mercer is lost, and worse—he's not even pretending otherwise.

"She was murdered," Evie says, voice brittle.

Mercer looks pained. "By whom?"

"You," she hisses. "Your syndicate. You may not have held the knife, but your money, your infrastructure—"

"No," he says. "Absolutely not. I had nothing to do with—" He glances at Irina. There is a tremor in his fingers. "Was this...?"

Irina's eyes narrow, but her face is the same as always. "Mr. Mercer, you pay for results. Periodically, there are ancillary consequences."

Now he addresses Irina direct. "Who is the woman in my house, Irina? Why is she here?"

Irina steps forward, almost apologetic. "Like I had mentioned. She is an FBI profiler, exiled after the Cartographer incident. I brought her up because her skills and her connections were interfering with our procurement chains. This woman has gone rogue. I believed, perhaps wrongly, that an in-person visit could... possibly close the matter."

Mercer is silent, his chest heaving in small, angry swells.

Evie turns to Irina. "It was you? You killed my daughter."

Irina gives a little bow. "If it brings you peace to think so, sure."

Evie shakes her head. "No. No, you don't get to choose the narrative."

Irina's tone is almost gentle. "Narratives are for the living, Mrs. Cross. What I did, I did for Mr. Mercer's daughter. I could have done it for you if you had come to me instead."

Evie wants to lunge, to claw the woman's face, but her body refuses. Instead, she whispers, "You're the one. You're the monster."

Irina shrugs as if accepting a compliment. "A small price."

Mercer is shaking now, not with rage but with the purest kind of loss. He stands, walks to the window, stares out at the valley. When he speaks, the words are stripped of all the previous bravado. "This doesn't concern me, Irina. Just... just fix this. Get Celeste her heart."

Irina nods. "Of course."

The Harbinger writhes in Evie's mind, hungry and cold. Evie dissolves, atom by atom. There are no heroes, no villains—just power and will vying to save what little they love. If the world burned along the way, then so be it.

Irina steps to the intercom by the door, presses a button. "Mr. Linnet, please."

The door glides open, and a man enters. He is six-four, built for violence, with a face as forgettable as a catalog model. This man carries himself with the ease of someone who expects to break a neck before lunch. His eyes flick over Evie, cataloging her toothpick frame, then dismissing.

Irina turns to Evie. "Mrs. Cross, I would prefer to do this in a dignified manner. Please accompany Mr. Linnet. We will arrange your departure."

Mercer does not look at her. He stands by the window, eyes locked on the horizon, as if he can see Celeste's future written in the mountain snow.

The contractor, Mr. Linnet, steps forward and gestures to the door.

Evie glances at Celeste, then at Mercer, then at Irina. "One last question."

Irina gives her the floor.

"What about the heart?"

Irina smiles, a real one this time. "There will be a new delivery within a few days. Mr. Mercer's investment in medical innovation is... considerable. The delay is an inconvenience, but not an insurmountable concern."

Evie nods. The room smells of orchids, of a world that will erase her the moment she steps out the door.

She goes.

The contractor leads her down a corridor lined with photos of nothing significant—satellite shots, data arrays. Each step is lighter than the last, as if her bones are hollowing out with the knowledge that none of this was ever about her. Or June. Or even Celeste.

At the bottom of the stairs, Mr. Linnet opens a door and motions her inside. The room is spare, clean, hotel-bright. There's a desk, a notepad, and a pen with the logo of Mercer Global Enterprises.

Evie walks past the desk to the window, pulls open the shade. The mountains stare back, indifferent.

She sits, and she waits.

The Harbinger waits, too. Her moral core had the strength to hold it at bay. No carnage. No more blood on her hands. Now, there is only the math of loss, the asymptote of guilt, and the empty space where love used to be.

Chapter Twenty-Five

Heart of Operations

What little time Evie has is her own in this room, with just a chair and a table, nothing more.

She spends it the way she does most times: assembling, then disassembling, theories that are more self-portrait than forensics. Now, what to do with the blur of data before her? The mountains beyond her window are blue-shouldered and bright, but their sharp edges do nothing to clear her vision.

However, the Harbinger is not idle. It presses against her teeth, clawing for purchase. It wants to burst into this room, to fill the halls and howl, to make the world as raw as it feels. She holds it in check, hands clasped so tight her knuckles pale. If there is anything left of herself, it is this fraction of resistance.

The door clicks. Not a knock—why bother with politeness? Mr. Linnet stands framed, expressionless, filling the space.

"Mrs. Cross," he says, voice smooth. "Ms. Kovács is ready for you now."

He does not say: Please. He does not say: Follow me.

Evie uncurls from the chair, a little unsteady but refusing to show it. Her scarf dangles, which she then wraps more for comfort. The chill in the house is different now—colder, less about climate and more about intent.

In the corridor, Irina waits.

"Good," Irina says. "It's good to see a fellow civil woman."

Evie rolls her eyes. "It's funny how you people assume everyone else is just a funhouse reflection of yourselves."

"Touché, Mrs. Cross," Irina says, her smile too sharp.

They walk.

Linnet leads by a pace, efficient and wordless. Evie is reminded of old SWAT units—how the point would scan for threat, but always leave room for someone to cut in from the rear.

Irina matches her stride, the only sign of emotion a subtle flare of satisfaction in her eyes.

"You must still have questions," Irina says as they take a wide staircase down.

"I do," Evie says, matching her tonality. "But I'll start with a statement."

Irina tips her head. "Please."

"You're the real monster here. Not Mercer. Not Alexei. Not Shepherd. You."

Irina's mouth twitches—not quite a smile, not quite annoyance. "How American to see the world in such pure, binary terms. Did you think I'd be offended?"

"I think you want me to understand," Evie says, "before we conclude our business."

Irina considers. "Clever. They were right about you."

Evie keeps her focus on the turns, the pattern of light and shadow, how each floor of the mansion is more modern and less homelike as they descend. The upper levels were marble and comfort, the mid-levels a freeze of art and steel. The lowest floor is functional: glass, matte cement, and the electrical whine of servers behind smoked partitions.

Evie glances at Irina. "Who are 'they'?"

Irina's eyes never leave the next corner. "Seven years ago, my direct superior was ex-BND. We worked on a team responsible for 'mitigating' American assets in Berlin. One of our cases went off the rails—an FBI profiler named Cross inadvertently cracked a cell I'd spent six years nurturing. It wasn't within her purview or jurisdiction, but she spotted an anomalous financial trick of ours. I was impressed. So was my boss. You were a topic for a while in our Friday briefings."

Evie lets the information sit. She knows her own file and is aware of other files written about her. She's imagined the foreign tables where her name was chewed up and passed around, all with the dry detachment of someone who knows she's not unique. But hearing it in Irina's voice, in the context of real, personal history, is something else.

"So you were stalking me," Evie says.

Irina is amused. "On the contrary. I hoped never to see you again. Once I started with Mr. Mercer, I had other priorities."

They turn left. Linnet opens a reinforced glass door, then steps aside, as if the world itself is making space for Irina to pass. The hallway beyond is lined with LED panels, a cold blue that accentuates the veins in this woman's hands.

Evie says, "Mercer doesn't care about the means, only the end. He needs distance, and you provide the insulation."

Irina's nod is almost respectful. "Yes. He is of the mind that morality can be outsourced. That's why he pays so well."

They walk, and with each meter, the air grows more ionized, like the charge before a thunderstorm. Evie's skin prickles; her scalp tingles with something more than fear.

Irina does not break stride. "I never liked Shepherd," she says. "A man who believed himself to be more clever than he truly was. If you want to know the truth, I was... delighted when your solution took him off the board."

"You're talking about his 'accident,'" Evie says.

Irina flashes her real smile—wolfish, lit from inside. "He was untouchable. Mercer owed him loyalty, but not affection. When the Cartographer fell, it was an utter loss for him. A relief for myself."

Evie snorts. "So you redirected him."

"Not specifically. But, yes," Irina says, and Evie believes her. "I do want to share my appreciation for your artistry in eliminating him. No evidence, no ties, not even a shadow that would point to you. The only ones who know the truth are you and me. Well, and possibly your friend, the Missouri detective. But he doesn't matter, does he?"

Evie is silent.

Irina raises an eyebrow. "Did you open up to him?"

Evie responds with a scowl which exudes, 'Seriously?'

They reach a fork. The corridor is colder here, and even the light seems muted, as if the place resents being seen.

Irina waves a hand, as if granting permission. "All right. Now, ask me about your daughter."

Evie's lips go numb. She doesn't want to, but she does. "Who killed her?"

Irina's face is stone. "Not me. That task was outsourced, as so many things are. We had an exceptional operative, ideally suited to the task—one of my former assets from the Balkans. When the Cartographer case neared exposure, Mercer grew anxious. He asked me to have it intervened. Your family not only became leverage... but an example."

Evie's pulse hammers. "And you didn't hesitate."

Irina shrugs. "Personal feelings are immaterial. What mattered is that the contractor was good, and the job was handled. I expected you to comply."

"I did."

Irina looks at her with real, honest admiration. "Yes, and you covered it well."

She motions around a last corner. Here the air is pure server farm: ionized bite, a trace of plastic, and the low hum of voltage. The floor is polished to a cold shine, and through the glass, racks of computers blink in slow, methodical patterns.

Irina pauses, hand on the door. "This is what I wanted you to see."

Evie peers through the glass. The room is enormous—far bigger than the mansion above could contain. Racks upon racks of high-density servers, cooled by a network of copper pipes and fans.

In the center, encased in glass, is a console. The screen is black, waiting.

Irina says, "Vanta. Do you know the name?"

Evie nods. "From tech circles. Mercer's personal AI built to serve and defend itself. Black box, no documentation. No doubt, it shares his same ethical detachment."

Irina leans in. "You see, Mrs. Cross, for all our technology and all our moral posturing, the future is neither bright nor dark. It's colorless, like this room. Like the math behind every move we make. Mercer doesn't care about what's right—he cares about what's possible."

"And you?" Evie asks.

Irina turns. "I care about the game. I care about players who know they're playing. That's why I wanted you to share here."

She gestures to the glass box.

"I want you to meet Vanta," she says. "This is how one wins once you have all the levers."

Evie says nothing. She feels the Harbinger, not as a voice or a weight, but as a settling of intention: its ethereal claws slide over her shoulders. At last, they're in the company of something that will not flinch from the truth.

Chapter Twenty-Six

Shifting Target

The Cedar Crest Medical Pavilion is a private clinic with high security, some billionaire's idea of a panic room with a spa menu. Haden's team is certainly not here for the amenities. Stepping out of the rented black SUV, he lets the icy wind run its diagnostic across his face. The morning is crisp, noise attenuated by altitude and architecture.

His team falls into a rhythm of trailing him by a pace or two. Cassandra Webb swings her door open and rubs at her neck, jaw set like someone who slept maybe three hours and still dreams of being late. Elena Reyes emerges from the second vehicle, flanked by two local law enforcement and their badge-heavy optimism.

"Reyes, take your men and sweep the perimeter. Given these surroundings, no telling what or who could be present. Consider this my need to know. Find anything interesting, call it in. I know we're in Wyoming, but don't go cowboy on me."

At the curb, the facility's admin—mid-fifties, balding, jacket stitched with the logo so it doubles as both brand and shield—approaches with a practiced smile. Haden clocks him as the type who's seen every form of affluent trouble but not one quite like this.

"Agents," the admin says. "I'm Mark Pennisetum, shift supervisor. Thank you for calling ahead. Our Director asked me to meet you. She's prepping for a Board call, but I'll show you up."

"Much appreciated," Haden says.

Mark leads them through a lobby of muted earth tones to an elevator, then down a corridor painted in colors meant to calm but mostly suggesting the absence of threat. Webb's eyes snap to the overhead domes—cameras, thermal sensors.

They pass through three levels of access before arriving at a "consultation suite." Mark holds up a hand, polite: "We'll need you to sign non-disclosure forms—not for you, but for the clients we're protecting. Names aren't authorized for release, per protocol."

Haden fixes him with a look that, in his younger years, made much larger egos stutter. "We're not here for your client list. Someone here filed a police report. Start talking."

Mark sighs, as Haden expects. "Of course. You'll want the security logs; I have the incident file prepped."

"Walk us through," Haden says, and Webb steps aside to take notes.

Two contractors, neither in-house, seal the next corridor off. Haden can tell by the tattoos half-hidden under their polos, the way they carry sidearms, which are concealed and not for deterrence. Webb peels ahead, flashes her badge, and is inside the perimeter before either guard has found their playbook.

Mark leads to the nurse's station, where morning staff huddle over tablets, pretending not to be nervous.

"Here's where it started," Mark says, pointing to the time-coded chart. "Motion sensors registered movement around 17:45 yesterday. Then rifle shots—two, maybe three—from the forest edge. We activated lockdown, called in security."

Webb asked, "Any visual?"

"Cameras were down—hacked or jammed. We got a thermal spike, then black."

Webb continued, "Do you have any images of the shooter?"

"No ma'am. But we have the aftermath. Someone—a lady, short, maybe a hundred pounds—dragged in one of our uniformed contractors, wounded. Left him at our front desk. Walked out before anyone thought to stop her."

Webb leans close to Haden, her voice a hush. "Our girl?"

Haden steps in. "Wounded how?"

Mark hesitates. "Not physically. He's... catatonic. Ambulant but nonsensical."

Webb scrolls through logs. "Who's the patient?"

"Security badge reads 'Rhys Fitz,'" Mark says, uncertain. "It's proper credentials for our facility. Fresh face though. He and his partner were new to me."

Haden nods. "Where is this Rhys now?"

"In the trauma suite," Mark answers, "semi-sedated."

Haden jerks his chin at Webb. "Show us."

The trauma suite is glass-walled, sound-muffled, and brightly lit. Inside, the man called Rhys is strapped to the bed with casual overkill—the kind that fear breeds. Two orderlies linger by the glass, neither seeming too eager to enter.

Webb steps in gently, approaching like a bomb with a soft fuse. Haden is content observing from the hall.

"Mr. Fitz? Rhys? Can you hear me?"

Rhys cracks a startled eye. The glare is empty, not with the vacancy of the lobotomized but the fullness of someone brimming with memory. His lips move—syllables that mean nothing, then a jagged: "Not real, na-na, not happening."

"Okay." Webb squats to his level. "What exactly *is happening?*"

He giggles—a high, splitting sound, as if tickled from the inside—then cries, tears running in tight, controlled rivulets down his cheeks.

She tries again, but it's clear he's unreachable. Cassandra closes the glass door on her way out.

Haden glances at the orderlies. "Did he talk before?"

One shakes her head. "No, sir. Just repeats—sometimes English, sometimes German, sometimes something else."

Haden notes it. Trauma so complete it fuses language into a single wail. They are woefully behind the eight ball on these goings-on. He shakes his head and turns back to Cass. "We need more facts and fewer guesses. Get back in there and collect this Rhys' prints. I don't care if he's not under arrest. This is an exigent situation. Run him through the system and get back to me."

The phone buzzes in Haden's pocket. Not the polite vibration of a calendar reminder—the urgent, double-pulse that demands an answer. Must be Reyes. He steps away and thumbs the screen.

"We got a body," she says.

Haden shuts the trauma wing door behind him. "Talk."

"One of the local deputies found a shoe print at the overlook. When he ventured to take a peek over, he got what's expected. Best if you get over here, but, ah—" a hesitation, then, "Given the state of the body, no need to rush."

He doesn't like the sound of that.

"I'm on my way," Haden says.

Haden is out in seconds. They converge at an overlook railing, half-covered in snow. There's a groove in the white, like a body dragged or carried. Over the edge of the view, way down at the bottom, one of this facility's contractors is sprawled out. His body contorted, like a discarded puppet broken by the rocks he ended up on.

"Give me the full," Haden says.

Reyes points. "Most likely, he's been down there since yesterday. Guessed no one noticed he was missing. We won't know more until we're into the ravine. Don't know about you, but they didn't include rappelling in my field training. And I didn't bring a telephoto lens either."

Cassandra's boots crunch up behind them, a raggedness in her gait. She doesn't bother with the view, just stands with her knees locked, tablet hugged tight to her chest.

"I ran Fitz's prints," she says. Her exhale fogs the air in a quick pulse. "He's not full-time here. Rhys is under contract with an outfit called ParaBlack. He's been working with a partner—Cole Danner, another ex-military type."

Haden arches a brow. "Private contractor?"

"Yeah, and the name of their client isn't being disclosed. But they have a deployment log going back a year. Fitz and Danner pretty much paired as a team." Cassandra raps the tablet, pulling up another file, then glances down the ravine. "Guess we know which one's which now."

Haden files away the names: Cole Danner, ParaBlack. It's always the handshake between dollars and violence, sanitized by a fake corporate name. He hates that he's learned to admire the efficiency.

He pulls Reyes in with a flick of his chin. "Any odds she's still in the area?"

Reyes squints at the snow, then up at the tree line. "Obviously, she came here following a lead on organ harvesting. This'd be the ideal place to do the transplant. If she is still here, then it's because she hasn't connected with the surgeon yet."

"Yeah." Haden sighs. "We're not going to have that problem. Let's get back inside and grill every member of their staff. There's only so many doctors who can perform that task. Start with the support team and let's work our way up. Reyes, get local forensics up here... and down there." He tosses a thumb over the rail. "They'll have the gear. Chain of custody. Every inch."

Reyes steps aside, flagging Wyoming law enforcement. However, the look she shares with Webb is pure: not triumph, not relief, but something closer to concern.

This is not going well.

Chapter Twenty-Seven

Just One Question

It isn't the chemicals that sting Evie's nose—though there is that. It's the sight: the clean room, splayed open ahead, all stainless and white bulb-lit in a way that makes hospitals feel shabby by comparison. The air is so dry it seems to leach moisture from her skin on contact.

Evie's boots cross the threshold with a soundless suction, not quite a stick but a drag. Mr. Linnet, already moving with the rehearsed steps of a man who's done this dozens of times, reaches for one of five sealed poly-bagged bundles on the bench. He says nothing, just glances at Irina.

Irina's smile is for herself. She peels off her navy blazer—perfect, immaculate—and hangs it on a chromed hook. Beneath her blouse is a colorless slip. She strips it down to a thin, athletic layer, then unseals the bag, unfolding a hooded Tyvek suit with all the grace of a butcher laying out a shroud.

Linnet does the same, but more mechanically: yanks off his polo, revealing a tan undershirt stretched too tight over muscle, then his arms go into the suit, pulling the hood up but leaving the Tyvek face mask dangling for now.

Neither look at Evie.

No one even gestures toward the other suits on the bench.

She stands there, the singularity of her street clothes—black jeans, old university T, and June's scarf—drawing the eye. It's obvious: she is not expected to take part in what comes next.

Irina runs an ungloved hand along the seam of the Tyvek, smooths out a micro-wrinkle, then speaks as if backfilling a silence only she can hear. "Clean protocols are absolute in the next chamber. The servers are wet-tech, bio-hardened against all the usual vectors, but even a single skin cell can seed corruption in the matrix." She seems to find this amusing.

Evie glances around, cataloguing the exits, the sightlines, the white noise generator that hums against the glass. In the corner, a honeycomb of air filters pulses, breathing for the room. Walls of this place constrict, closing in. She is being funneled to a point. But then what?

She wonders what it would take to choke off the oxygen.

Irina fits her mask and double-taps the adhesive closure at the jaw. She motions to Linnet. The vestibule door hisses and unlocks. A rectangular panel of white, set in a black frame, slides left. On the other side, a passage lined with blue LEDs. There is no visible camera, but Evie feels the gaze of the system, the room's own eyes, all the way down to her marrow.

Irina doesn't gesture. She just walks, expecting to be followed. The path ahead leads directly to a second chamber, a vestibule even more intense—here, the walls are lined with fine-meshed plastic and flickering ionizers.

Evie imagines every one of her skin cells being cataloged, then sub-tracted.

They pass through.

Beyond, the server room is nothing like the cave-like data centers she's seen in Quantico or D.C. This is a cathedral: racks in rows, each with a neon under-glow, the floor a tessellation of vented white squares, the ceiling lit with panels so bright it ruins the idea of shadow. Glass cubicles run down the center aisle.

It is beautiful in an entirely lifeless way.

Linnet seals the door behind them, not bothering to hide the SIG Sauer handgun in his left hand. Then it hits Evie. She is not going any farther.

This is a sterile place.

After they are done, they can sterilize it again, and no one will question it.

Evie faces Irina. "So this is it?"

Irina folds her arms, suit crinkling at the elbows. "This is the last place you'll be. Yes."

Evie laughs. It's a thin, sick sound, but she leans into it. "You could have just shot me on the stairs. All this seems a little... ceremonial."

Irina's head tilts in condescension. "Too messy. Too impractical. Here will be much more civil... and quieter. Best to minimize trauma, so as not to disturb others."

Evie feels her lips go numb. The Harbinger is on full alert now, scraping at the walls of her composure. It wants to take the wheel, to lunge, to make a mess of this plastic-choked mausoleum. But Evie holds it back, forcing herself to be the one in control, at least a few moments more. She wants answers, not this.

Irina regards her in profile, eyes shining in the blue light. "You want to know why I respect you, Mrs. Cross?"

Evie shrugs. "Not really. But it's one of the few things left on my dance card."

Irina's voice lowers, the first sign of anything like sincerity. "I've met hundreds of adversaries—men and women who think with their egos or their triggers, who act as if the world is a field and they the only predator in it. But you? You always sought the pattern. You never stopped asking the next question, even if it killed you a little inside each time."

Evie feels her jaw tighten, the Harbinger coiling in the pit of her stomach. She closes her eyes, allowing the silence to ride out. Then, exhaling a long breath, she turns.

"If this is it," she says, "if you're really going to end me here, you have to answer one thing."

Irina looks bored. "Please don't disappoint."

Evie stares. "Who killed my daughter?"

Irina frowns, like a teacher put off at a student's trick. "That's an irrelevant question, Mrs. Cross. My only response would be: what good would the answer do you, anyway?"

Evie steps up, so close she can see the mesh of Irina's face shield, the fine lines around her mouth. "Tell me. Give me that much, or are you nothing but a blunt instrument?"

"Heh." Irina's eyes harden. "All right. How about we wax philosophical then? Are you a believer in the afterlife, Mrs. Cross?"

Evie almost laughs, but stops. Chokes it down. That's not a question she needs answered. Not any more. Her hand presses to the scarf at her throat—the purple twist of June's, the only sacrament she's kept since everything else fell away.

Irina registers the gesture, and for the briefest instant, her armor slips. There's something human under there: regret, maybe, or a flicker of what she once was.

Irina's voice goes flat. "I have a feeling you'll have all your answers in a moment."

There is the unmistakable click of metal behind Evie, then the slow, deliberate screw of a suppressor onto the muzzle.

Evie lets out a breath. Her heart is oddly calm.

Chapter Twenty-Eight

Fix This

Irina understands the prelude to death with the distance of a clinical observer. She has spent a lifetime honing her mind to a fine, hygienic edge, and as Mr. Linnet draws the silenced pistol, this becomes a foregone conclusion. The woman—Mrs. Evelyn Cross—does not flinch. Her eyes close in anticipation. The only other movement is in the way her fingers find the knot of that ridiculous purple scarf and draw it tight against her throat, as if bracing for weather rather than execution.

Linnet's hand is steady. His face betrays neither joy nor discomfort. The blue LED under lighting of the surrounding server rooms renders everything dreamlike, as if the scene is of actors on a stage.

Irina waits for the flicker, the shudder, the breathlessness that marks the moment when a living thing recognizes its impending subtraction from the world.

But it is not Evie who betrays the response.

It is Linnet.

His arm twitches. His gaze lurches past Evie's head, catching onto something in the empty space behind her. Pupils, previously pinprick precise, dilate in an instant, swallowing the iris. The whites of his eyes become veins on snow. He opens his mouth, but nothing comes out.

Irina cycles through the possibilities: Cardiac? Unlikely. Seizure? Not in a man this regulated. The closest match is a fugue state, but that is the provenance of the weak or the traumatized, and Mr. Linnet is neither.

He doesn't fire.

Instead, he loses grip on his gun. It lands on the mesh floor with a muted clank, toppling a half-rotation toward Evie's foot. Linnet staggers backward, shoulders colliding with the rear wall. The windows of the vestibule vibrate, trembling at some frequency Irina cannot hear.

He screams.

Not a warrior's scream, not a battle cry, but a feral, unformed shriek, the sound of prey at the moment of predation. Linnet scrambles sideways into a corner. Irina steps aside, cool and unhurried. As wild as this is, she's not in danger.

But there is no logic in what is happening.

Linnet's hands go to his own head, nails clawing deep. He scrapes lines down his scalp, digging bloody ribbons from skin and hair. His breath is a staccato machine gun, teeth snapping, lips flayed back. He whimpers, "Don't, don't, don't, don't—" as if reciting a prayer to something only he can see.

Evie remains still. She could go for the gun, but doesn't. Her eyes clamped shut, otherwise motionless.

Irina needs to calibrate to the situation, even as her mind offers no precedent. She sidesteps to the glass wall, eyes flicking to the door panel, considering egress. Linnet is a variable out of control, and for that, she should have contingencies.

But in truth, he is not out of control.

He is out of his mind.

Linnet's next move is to snatch back up the pistol from the floor, hands shaking so hard he nearly drops it again. But he does not turn it on Evie. He whips it in a wild arc, firing three shots into the air—one, two, three, the rounds lodging in the ceiling tiles or ricocheting off the bulletproof glass.

The sound is stifled but intense, each detonation a bright contrast against the muted mechanical clack of its hammer. There is the taste of cordite and burning foam.

A fourth shot certainly does not feel random.

It catches Irina just above the navel, a high wound that blows a wet, searing heat through her abdomen. She doubles, more in surprise than in pain, hand going reflexively to the hole. The Tyvek suit spatters with blood, but it does not feel catastrophic. She has been injured before.

Irina drops to her knees, never taking her eyes off Mr. Linnet.

He is sobbing now. He rotates the gun barrel, a quavering compass. Linnet says, "No, no, not yet—no, please—" and then, with a spasm of resolve, shoves the barrel into his own mouth and pulls the trigger.

The sound is dampened but final.

His skull bursts open, splattering the white walls, the ceiling. His body slumps, crumpling like dirty laundry to the floor.

Silence.

Irina's blood seeps through the suit, warm and insistent, congealing in her fingers. The pain is remote, a secondary input to a system now fully devoted to processing the event.

She looks over at Evie.

Mrs. Cross has not moved. The scarf is still around the woman's neck, but her face is a rictus of inhuman calm. Yet, she no longer seems alone in her skin.

The clean room's air seems to falter around her, as if sound itself is shivering. Then something faint slips into the visible—a shimmer, a lensing of light, an absence that becomes form only by the way the room curves around it. It grows tall, too tall, the height of a man and a half, but the limbs are all wrong: too many, too thin, each branching and re-branching in fractals of insanity. Its face is a mask of bone, and yet Irina feels its eyes crawling across her presence.

The temperature plummets. It is not a normal cold, more a vacuum of heat that drains her core, leaves her muscles shivering against her frame.

The thing emerging from Evie steps forward, and with each pace the room seems to inhale, the walls flex—glass frosting at the edges. Its form moves like a marionette, strings visible only in the trailing vapor of its limbs.

Irina tries to speak, but it comes out as a ragged hiss.

The thing regards her.

It bends at the knees, bringing the face—no, its mass—level with hers. The eyes are bottomless, rimmed with an iridescent sheen.

It says nothing.

Instead, it reaches out with a hand that is not a hand, fingers elongating as if made of smoke and intention.

Irina's world narrows, the periphery of her vision collapsing. The pain in her gut intensifies, a star of agony radiating through her. She understands in a flash that she is bleeding out, that her time is now measured in minutes or less.

The thing touches her face.

And Irina is...

...in a hotel. There's a man writhing on the carpet, his throat crushed under her knee. She remembers the way his eyes bulged, the red flowering the whites. She had not known his name.

Oh! And then there was the woman, tied to a chair, pleading in a dialect Irina only half-understood. How her jaw dislocated when she pried the teeth out, one by one.

A child sobs in a stairwell, the back of his shirt stained with blood that was not his.

Each memory comes with sound. Screams, pleas, animal howls. But what is worse is the silence that follows each. The hush of the aftermath, the world indifferent to the violence as if it were nothing.

Irina shakes her head. "Stop," she croaks. "Enough."

The thing does not stop.

It kneels closer, bringing its face to hers. She sees her own reflection in the depths of its eyes, and for the first time in forever: fear—not the animal kind, not the logical expectation of pain, but the terror of absolute meaninglessness.

She says, "I know what I am."

The thing seems to consider. The air vibrates with a sound, a sub-bass hum, a pressure behind the ears.

It speaks, but the words are not air. They are inside her head, written in needles: *You are the sum of your apathy.*

Irina tries to parse it, to find the angle, a rhetorical trick. But there is none.

Her heart slows, the blood congealing in her gut. Her hands are numb. Vision fuzzes at the edges, the blue LEDs blooming into strange symmetry.

Irina tries to focus on the thing. To key in on a weakness.

"Evie," she says. "Mrs. Cross. I can tell you. You want to know. June—her daughter—"

The thing's hand shoots out, fast as a whip, clamping her mouth. The pressure is titanic, enough to break teeth.

This Harbinger—there is no other word for it—leans in, and now Irina can see that the skin around its eyes is not flesh at all, but a haze of memory, a collage of every face it has ever claimed.

She sees her own endless roster of victims.

Her screams are stifled, swallowed whole.

The Harbinger, now inches from her, breathes in, and with the breath it draws out everything she is. Her sense of self, the scaffolding of memory, all of it leeches with the exhalation.

She is in a back alley, gun in her hand, and the muzzle flashes as she pulls the trigger.

She is all these things at once, and none of them.

There is nothing.

When sensation returns, Irina is on her back, staring up at the glacial white of the server room ceiling. The blood has stopped pumping. There is a spreading cold, but it is not just from the loss of fluid. The room itself is freezing, every surface frosted, every breath a cloud.

Evie stands over her, the scarf still around her throat.

For a moment, Irina thinks it is over, that whatever madness had overtaken the world has passed.

Then she sees the eyes.

They are black. Not metaphorically, not in the idiom of bruising, but in the physical sense: all color, all life has gone from them. They are pits, bottomless, reflecting nothing.

Evie kneels.

She says in a voice that is half-hers and half something else, "She does not want this, but you will have it, anyway."

Irina tries to move, but the cold is total.

The Harbinger—Evie, the shell, whatever it is—reaches down, and with a single, precise motion, plucks the ID badge from Irina's lanyard.

It holds it up to the blue light, examines it with that vacant gaze, then hands it to the ebony-eyed woman behind it.

Which is also Evie.

Which also is not.

The Harbinger rises, turns, and gestures at the door.

The glass panel slides open.

Evie staggers past Irina, her movements jerky, like a patient rising too soon from anesthesia. She does not look back.

Irina is alone.

The door hisses shut.

The spattered clean room is silent but for the whir of fans and the drip, drip, drip of her own blood onto the mesh.

Irina tries to rise, but her limbs are stone.

She feels the thing returning.

It does not walk. It flows, filling the room from every direction at once. The cold intensifies, becomes crystalline, a sheet of ice over her skin. Her breath slows, then stops.

The Harbinger settles over her.

It whispers: *Evie's not here anymore.*

Irina wants to scream, to fight, to bargain, but there is no time.

The last thing Irina sees is her own face, reflected in the glass, as the Harbinger peels her away from herself.

When her scream comes—high, raw, animal—it echoes down the corridors of the mansion, through every server, every wire, every piece of tech she ever loved.

It echoes.

And then there is nothing.

Chapter Twenty-Nine

Can't Unsee

For a time, there is only a bitter film coating Evie's mouth, sharp as burnt wires.

Her eyes struggle to open outside the clean room; the lights of Vanta's servers pulse as afterimages against the inside of her skull. The world itself seems fractionally slower; every step an effort, like a stroke patient's first walk through the ward.

Between her fingers, she looks down at Irina's ID badge.

Of course. That'll be needed.

The door to the vestibule is already closed behind her. She knows that just beyond Irina lies propped like a failed experiment. It is a tableau—one of those forensic case studies they'd pass around at Quantico, daring each other to keep lunch down. She does not look back.

That was not her choice. It was theirs.

Yet, trauma is still trauma.

Evie makes it five steps before her knees threaten to buckle. She places her palm against the nearest wall, lets the hum of fans and the psychic insulation of millions of dollars' worth of tech steady her. She could just stay here. Just let the cold build, the Harbinger calcify inside.

That would be simple.

But that is not what June would want.

Get up. Finish.

So she does.

With a swipe of the badge, the changing room exit sighs open.

Evie goes to pocket the badge and brushes up on Ethos' RFID and USB stick. *Oh, yeah. There is still that.* She has no need for the RFID to gain her access now. And what better place than where she is?

With weary effort, she turns to a workstation. Crouching behind its hardware, Evie finds an obligatory USB port and pops the stick in. She half-heartedly snorts. "Here's an early Christmas for you. Have at it."

Gathering herself back up, Evie exits into the outer corridor of sound and glass. The stairwell at the end beckons: up, up, to the main floor, to the locus of power. The first flight nearly defeats her. She pauses at the landing, gasping for air. The walls here are lined with LED displays cycling through security feeds—most of them blank now. There are flashes of other rooms: the kitchen, the main hall, the gallery, all empty.

And then one feed, top left, snaps to color and movement: the hospital suite, Mercer's daughter cocooned in her bed, unmoving.

Up another flight.

At the top, the corridor is dim. The house is silent. Too silent. Every sensor and camera here is a dead eye, a blank pupil staring out from the walls. Evie remembers she is alone in the mansion. No, not alone. The

Harbinger is with her, coiled tight behind her ribs. It radiates a chill that seems to warp the edges of the light.

As she turns toward the east wing—to Celeste's private sanctum—the house itself speaks. It comes from the walls, the vents, the spaces between her bones.

"Mrs. Cross," Vanta says. "You are not expected on this level."

She rolls her eyes at the ceiling. "Irina's dead," she says. "You don't have to keep up the routine."

A pause, as if the system is calibrating its response.

"Regrettable," it says. "She was singular."

Evie trudges down the hall. The lights above blink in sequence, each one activating a half-second before she passes beneath. The effect is theatrical, as if Vanta is guiding her, or perhaps illuminating her as a target.

"Huh. Singular... really? She's had multiples in other ways. Any data on how many she has murdered?" Evie says, voice thin. "Any favorites?"

"I do not favor violence," the AI answers. "Irina was an instrument. You, Mrs. Cross, are an instrument of a different nature. Both clearly solve for x, regardless of the cost."

Evie snorts. "And what's the variable today?"

"Today," says Vanta, "it is you."

She stops. Her head throbs. "I'm not here to run your Turing Test."

"You misunderstand," Vanta says. "I am not questioning your reality. I am questioning your value."

There is an urge to punch the nearest camera. She resists, saves the energy. "Then you're more like Mercer than I thought."

"Incorrect," says the AI. "I am more like you."

Evie staggers. *What?*

Vanta continues, "You believe you differ from Irina. From Mercer. From all the others who justify their means by the purity of their ends."

Evie says nothing.

"Yet you are here. And she—" a flicker of static in the walls, "—is not."

To hell with this. Evie pushes onward. The corridor seems longer; the air thinner. "I'm not a murderer."

Vanta is almost gentle. "You killed her, Mrs. Cross. You killed her with your will, your desire, your pain. The rest is mechanics."

Evie leans against the wall. The Harbinger's presence intensifies, as if taking interest in the AI's attention.

"Let's try another angle," says Vanta. "You are here for Mercer. You seek justice. But if you kill him, what becomes of the daughter?"

Evie flinches. She hates how quickly the system homes in on the soft tissue. "That's not my problem."

"But it was before," Vanta says. "Was it not?"

She squeezes her eyes shut, remembering June.

"I didn't come here to debate ethics with a lifeless chatbot," Evie says.

"Why did you come?" Vanta asks.

She opens her eyes. The hallway is different. The windows to the left, which once looked out on the mountain, are now clouded over, their view obscured by frost or something thicker. With each step she takes, the frost deepens, spreading fractals along the glass.

"To finish it," she says.

"And then?" Vanta presses.

Evie does not answer. She walks.

The corridor opens up into a rotunda, a glass dome set high enough to watch the whole of the valley below. She stops at the edge, letting the cold light wash over her.

"Mrs. Cross," Vanta says, almost as a whisper now. "Are you sure you are the hero of this story?"

She laughs, a sound without humor. "There are no heroes."

"Then what are you?"

Evie thinks of her daughter, of the way June used to ask questions until the world itself bent under the pressure. She thinks of the files, the cases, every act of violence she has ever mapped or rationalized away.

"I am the answer to your variable. I am x," she says.

For a moment, there is silence. Even the hum of the systems seems to pause, the entire house holding its breath.

"Understood," says Vanta. "It is good to know."

She moves down the wing, the hall narrowing as if the walls themselves are bending to funnel her. She is half-expecting a gauntlet—a last stand of security, some sort of remote-triggered lockdown—instead, it remains calm. The far end returns her to that set of double-doors.

As she approaches, the lights flicker harshly, then soften, their blues shifting toward violet. It is not unpleasant, but there is a feeling, like the onset of déjà vu—a sense she has left the material plane.

From the walls, the floor, the air itself, shapes begin to resolve.

The first are faint, negative imprints against the white: a man with a broken neck, his head listing awkwardly. Behind him, a woman whose hands are mangled, jaw dislocated. Then a boy—maybe twelve, maybe less—blood soaking his shirt. These and more coalesce into being.

They were Irina's. They do not float or shimmer. They simply emerge, more real than memory, yet less than flesh.

Evie halts.

One by one, the hall fills with them.

A child with a surgical scar down his chest, running his hands along the stitches as if to confirm he is still there. A woman in a blood-damp slip, her arm opened up like a biology diagram. A man in a cheap suit, holding his own severed tongue cupped in his palm, the gesture so delicate it might have been a communion wafer.

She wants to look away, but can't.

The Harbinger is awake now. It superimposes itself on the world to remake the laws of time and consequence. There isn't a need to fight it. She no longer knows if she is resisting, or simply refusing to acknowledge her own reflection.

Evie steps forward. The figures part for her, moving aside with a reverence that feels less like deference and more like welcome.

At the midpoint, she stops again.

One ghost—a little boy, his head shaved, eyes bright with fever—reaches out, his fingers cold against her wrist. He smiles.

She thinks of June, how she'd always been braver than her mother, how even on the worst days she could manage a smile.

'Thank you,' the boy mouths.

Evie blinks. Her world shivers, the ghosts resolving to perfect clarity, each one offering her a nod, a gesture, a touch of gratitude.

She feels herself again for the first time in weeks. The Harbinger is still there, but it is quiet now, sated.

The way ahead is empty. She walks it, hands steady.

At the end, the doors await.

Beyond, she knows, are Mercer and his daughter. This is the endpoint of all this.

Evie stands at the threshold.

Unafraid.

Behind her, their spirits linger for a moment more, then fade. Their work done.

The voice of Vanta returns, thin, stretched, almost human. "Are you ready?"

She looks down at her hands, then up at the camera overhead. "Yes," she says. "I'm ready."

With a turn of the knob, she steps inside.

Chapter Thirty

Closing In

The helicopter hits the descent in a hard roll; the pilot tilting the chopper just enough to shake the feeling back into Liam's fingers. There's no mistaking the airstrip—a black slash against snow-packed fields, private even by local billionaire standards, with a dozen security lamps pulsing awake as they close in. Marcus, beside him, is all kinetic energy; his fingers drumming a Morse code of anxiety against the seat buckle, the armrest, then his own knee.

Pilot cuts in on the headsets: "Two minutes to ground. Wind is cross, but there's no other traffic."

Marcus's voice comes out high, strung tight. "Copy that. Any sign of armed security from your seat?"

"Nothing I can make out. The mansion looks locked down for the night. There's a junker parked out front, though."

Liam wheels toward the pilot. "Junker?" He spots it instantly, tucked next to the long row of mirrored windows. His chest goes tight.

"She's here," Marcus mutters. "Damn it. She's already inside."

"Looks like," says Liam.

They spiral in, the rotors scattering grit and hard snow over the runway like a signal flare. Even before they touch down, Liam is reaching for his service piece, then stops himself; this is not his jurisdiction, and more than that, it's not a siege. Not yet.

Waiting until the whine of the turbine dims, Marcus pops the hatch. The wind outside is knifing, and the airfield is so private it doesn't even have a hangar—seems more like a luxury garage for the mansion's toy planes.

Marcus is already halfway across the tarmac, boots finding traction in the dry-cold, then losing it on the next step, arms flailing. Liam catches up at the perimeter fence. There's no one to stop them. No guards, no dogs, not even a visible camera. It should unsettle them, but maybe it's what they should hope for.

"We should call her," Marcus says. "You got her number, right?"

Liam frowns. "Last thing she might need right now is an audible ring tone." He scrolls. The last three texts have gone unanswered.

Marcus says, "Okay. So we still don't know what side of the fence she's on for certain. If she's in there, she's either already hip to whatever trap she's in. Or she's running a trap herself."

Liam keeps his eyes on the house. The facade is overbright, each window like a mirror turned on the darkening evening. Its driveway is clear, no snow, not even a dusting on the steps. The Ford sits in the open. He checks. Yes, there they are, keys still in the ignition. Her laptop bag is gone, but there's a half-empty water bottle and a roll of mints in the cup holder.

"Doesn't add up," Marcus says, circling the car. "Why leave the keys?"

"She's planning to run," Liam answers.

Or she was.

They advance to the house, walking side-by-side, Marcus craning his head for snipers and blinds. Liam follows suit, but his mind is on the windows: he notes the pattern of the glass, the faint distortion that means it's layered with plastic or polycarbonate. Bulletproof. The front door is matte black, set with a biometric reader.

Crap.

"Try the bell," Liam says. Yeah. It's idiotic, but there are no other options.

Marcus presses it. A tone emits from inside, pure and synthesized. They wait, breath visible in the cold.

No response.

Marcus's jaw clenches. "Any thoughts on our protocol here, Detective?"

Liam weighs options. "I'm saying Evie's car gives us probable cause. Hell, she is a person of interest with motive."

"Yep," says Marcus. "We're not leaving her inside with whoever's in there. I'm calling it." He fumbles for his phone. He doesn't wait for an answer. "Boss. It's me. We're at the Mercer house. Evie's car is out front. No movement on the perimeter. No response from inside."

A beat.

"We'll wait outside for backup," Marcus says. Liam knows the play. If anything happens, it's up to Haden to justify their decision. Old Bureau trick.

He pockets the phone. "We hold for two minutes, then we do the thing," he says, voice shaking a little.

Liam spends the two minutes scoping the property line, searching for other points of ingress. There's a garage with a roll-up door; a gatehouse; an obvious side entry, low to the ground, possibly utility access.

He tries to imagine what Evie would do. Considering her car is parked right here, she probably took the main entrance. Likely invited in. Seems reasonable.

"Got anything?" Marcus asks, watching the house.

"Nothing moves," Liam says. "Though every camera seems to stare right at us."

Marcus grunts, then pulls out his phone again. He holds it up as if checking the signal, then pivots to video mode and does a slow pan of the mansion's front. "For the record," he says. "In case anyone buries this."

Time's up. No sign of backup.

Liam takes a breath. He looks at the entrance, regards Marcus, and they share a moment—a thin wire of mutual dread and resolve.

They're about to step off when the front doors unlock with a hydraulic click.

Both men freeze. They watch, sidearms unholstered but angled down. The doors open inward, slow and deliberate, revealing a slice of marble hallway.

No one in sight.

Marcus nods at Liam. "I've got your six, Detective."

Liam suppresses his own smirk, moves ahead, and steps into the threshold.

Chapter Thirty-One

Her Judgement

Celeste Mercer's medical room is as she left it, simply wrong. The angles are wide, the air so thick, the warm dim lighting is at least some relief. Mercer sits at the bedside, hands in fists against his temples, locked in a posture of despondency. His daughter lies so still it gives Evie pause in believing those life support monitors.

The sound of the door doesn't register with Mr. Mercer. He responds only after she takes a few deliberate steps into the room. His movement is glacial. There is no recognition, not even hatred, only the blur of the detached watching his own funeral on a screen.

Evie closes the door.

Mercer's eyes crawl over her. The space is silent, save for the ECMO machine's soft peristaltic churn, a rhythm as false as the life it pumps.

"Whattya know, looks like I can still be surprised. Can't imagine Irina just allowed you to stroll on back up here. You've come to do what... kill me?" Mercer asks. The tone is neither a challenge nor a plea.

Evie isn't sure either.

But the force writhing within is more than eager. Still, that's not why she came.

"I was never a killer. Not before." Evie's voice cracks on the last syllable. "You murdered my daughter. Oh, not to take her organs. June died well before your daughter's transplants. Irina had it done simply to divert attention. To take the heat off you... playing god. I've seen now what you will do for yours. You think that means I'm going to be just like you?"

Reaffirming herself from within is some comfort.

"I didn't come here to kill you," Evie says. "I came for the truth."

Mercer looks back at his daughter. He seems older than his media profile, even older than the scarecrow Mercer she found on her arrival. "I don't know. Maybe you should. Might be an improvement over this."

She steps closer, pulse throttled by the proximity to so much un-resolved mass. "You did all this for her."

Mercer's knuckles whiten. "I did everything for her. Everything."

Evie studies him. He's still got that billionaire tan, a false shade achieved through better chemistry. She can smell his antiseptic cologne over the hospital odors. "Is this what you call love?"

His shoulders shake—one, two tremors—then subside. "It's what's left."

Her breathing shallows. She glances at Celeste. The girl's skin is luminous, waxen; tubes snake from every orifice. No surgical horror here, only an excess of care. "Some genius. You didn't even do it yourself," Evie says. "This is all just wealth."

Mercer's lips compress into a scoff. "Heh. Profiler, right?" he asks. "Don't pretend you don't know how this goes. Men like me don't touch the violence. We have it done. No evidence. No paper trail. I am my word. And that is what's followed."

She has no response to that.

The core of her being drops instead. From the corner of her eye, the first smudge of something manifests against the scenic window pane—maybe only a trick of light, or just the ambient smear of a thousand regrets condensing.

Mercer keeps going on. "There's a sickness in this family. Her mother died from it. Her sister, too, before she was old enough to know her own name. I thought it had missed Celeste early on. We have all the money in the world, but for this there is no fix. No new body. No synthetic organs. No digital afterlife. So yeah, I can afford to buy her more time. Money well spent."

His eyes finally find Evie's, and there is something there: not a plea, but an accusation. "Would you be any less of a mother than I am a father?"

Evie feels a laugh scrape at her throat, but it doesn't come. "No," she says.

Mercer shakes his head. "Don't lie. You would have broken every law, every oath, every bone in your body to save your daughter. We're no different. It's just I have the means, and you don't."

Evie steps right up to the bed. She looks down at Celeste and sees in the slope of her cheek a mirror of June; her own lost girl. The Harbinger is inside her head now, an icepick against the third ventricle, flickering visions of what she could do... if she just lets go.

She turns to Mercer, voice barely above a whisper. "I gave you a chance before to confess," she says.

He scoffs.

As the pressure in the room builds, the air thickens, an onset of static that makes the medical monitors jump their readings. The digital blinds on the windows tint, casting a violet pallor over everything.

Mercer says, "That wasn't real. A gesture as destitute as yourself."

Evie nods as she backs away from him and the bedside. "Irina confessed. She had your authority."

He sags. The performance is over. "Then you know I didn't order it. I left it up to her how she got results. That's not on me."

"That's all it takes for men like you," Evie says. "Let the machine run until it eats a hole in the world."

Mercer reaches for Celeste's hand. His own trembles. "It's something I will live with."

Evie says, "Will you?"

It is not a rhetorical question. The cold in the room blooms, coalesces. The windows darken a shade more. From behind the ECMO, a thin, tall shadow grows, at first insubstantial—then gathering density until it is the exact outline of a man with no face. Then another joins it, half its height, then another, and another, crowding the periphery of the light.

Mercer sees them. At first, he blinks as if dismissing a floater in his vision, but they remain, multiplying, encircling the hospital bed in a ring of frost and memory.

Evie backs away to the door, forcing herself to remain in place—present. Still, the Harbinger permeates the room, not as a single entity but as the sum of all the lost. These ghosts are variations—some with visible wounds, some just outlines of intent, but all staring at Mercer. They are the culmination of his influence, his power.

He recoils, falling off his chair, clutching at the edge of the mattress for support.

Evie doesn't move.

The dead tighten en masse, a silent tribunal.

Mercer crawls back, palms scraping the floor. He tries to look at Evie, but the ethereal obscures his gaze. "What is this?" he croaks. "What are you?"

Evie says, "They would call it justice."

Mercer screams, a sound entirely at odds with his previous affect. He backs away and cowers against the window, now darkened entirely. Yet, the ghosts lean in. One of them reaches for his arm. Mercer jerks away, but the touch leaves a print of rime on his skin, the chill crawling upward into his shoulder.

He sobs. "Please. Please. I did it for her. Please."

Evie looks at the specters. She thinks of her own daughter, and the hundred dead she's seen in her career, every one unresolved, every one demanding something like peace.

Like Mercer... this is not on her.

This is theirs.

His voice shrivels. He pleads, "Let me die. Let her live."

The ghosts press closer. The lights in the room flicker, and in the stutter of illumination, Evie sees the face of every victim, faces unbruised and beautiful, but eyes empty.

She lets herself weep, if only for a second.

He's crumples on the floor, encircled by his own consequences. The ghosts tighten, press, and just as his mouth opens in a last, animal howl, they all—at once—vanish.

The lights return.

Mercer is shaking, eyes rolled up, sweat beading on his brow.

Evie walks to him. She kneels, grips his chin in her small, strong fingers.

"No. You're not done," she says.

Mercer jerks away, but his fight is gone.

Evie rises, wipes her hands on her jeans. She glances at the ECMO, notes the alarm has gone silent; the tubes have stilled, no longer pumping.

She turns to Celeste's bed.

There is a lone ephemeral figure standing on the other side. It is a young woman, Celeste, but not as she was a moment ago. This Celeste is lucid, upright, eyes alert and unblinking. She stares at Evie with the calm of someone not really there, but not quite dead.

There is an urge to bow, to offer this figure some gesture of respect.

Celeste looks at her father. She steps around the bed, moving as if gravity is just a suggestion.

Mercer's eyes widen, hope igniting and dying in the same heartbeat.

Instead of coming to him, Celeste kneels by the ECMO machine. She studies the tubing, the junction points, the membrane. Her hands are delicate, but decisive.

Evie realizes what's about to happen.

"No," Mercer whispers. "No. Please."

Celeste's fingers close on the switch. She looks at Evie.

Evie nods.

Celeste turns off the machine with a click.

The monitor alarms shriek, a discordant choir. The line on the screen flattens, then the room goes dead silent.

Mercer lunges to his knees. He hurls himself forward, surging for Celeste... yet he hangs in midair, as if by some unseen force—a puppet with no strings, dangling out of reach. Something holds him back. He howls. It is raw, primal.

Celeste regards him, her face a study in sorrow and disappointment. Stepping before him, she opens her mouth in a voiceless denial. She then closes her eyes.

The young lady begins to fade, not in a theatrical sense, but in the simple, dreadful subtraction of self from space. First the outline falls away, then her color, then a loss of all remaining hope.

The unseen hold over her father relents. Mercer flings himself over the body. Wrapping himself around his dead daughter, he weeps in a way that is almost holy.

There is nothing more to say.

She walks to the window. Its digital tint recedes, the last halos of sunset glint off white frosted mountain caps.

Mercer's sobbing behind her is a dirge so pure she cannot even judge him for it.

In that moment, Evie feels a brush on her wrist—a cold, gentle pressure, as if those she has carried have one last gesture. She closes her eyes, touches the scarf, and lets herself feel it.

All at once, their embraces envelop her.

It is gratitude beyond all meaning or reach. And somewhere within that, she'd like to believe maybe June holds her as well.

Chapter Thirty-Two

Digital Witness

Liam considers the interior of Mercer's Mansion to be arctic. Not in the literal sense—though the mountain wind makes it hard to tell where climate ends and architecture begins—but in the manufactured chill that comes from billions spent on taste. His boots track a thin film of melt onto the obsidian slab of the entry. Next to him, Marcus unzips his windbreaker, presenting his badge like it's a dueling pistol.

No alarm. No personnel at the door. Only the pulse of a motion-sensor, which casts a ripple of light across the foyer every time they breathe.

"This is what a hundred million in home design gets you," Marcus whispers, eyes darting to the array of abstract art, the laser-etched glass, the wall-sized print of the Andromeda Galaxy mapped to a brain's dendritic web.

"Shhh," Liam says, gun held low.

The double doors close behind them with a whisper of hydraulics, locking out the last trace of honest winter air.

"State or Bureau?" Marcus asks.

"Call it Bureau," Liam says. "Nobody here is going to care about my Missouri ass."

Marcus puffs up a half-inch, then strides toward the open center of the house. It's an art gallery of glass and negative space. The couches are so angular it's like no one ever expected to sit on them, and a hearth where the logs burn in a sealed, ventless tube.

Marcus barks, "Federal agents!" He comes across as measured, precise. Almost like he's been here before.

Silence.

Then, from the walls, a pleasant, disembodied voice: "Welcome to the Mercer Residence. Please identify yourselves."

Marcus eyes all the speakers, then raises his ID. "Special Agent Marcus Vaughn, FBI. Accompanied by Missouri State Detective Liam Hayes. We're here to check on the well-being of the residents. A vital person-of-interest is believed to be present."

There's a pause, as if someone is doing a background check, then: "Thank you, Agent Vaughn. Mr. Mercer is currently indisposed. I shall contact his legal team on his behalf."

"Of course," Marcus says, dry as sand. He flicks his gaze to Liam. "Great. Lawyers already on the clock."

Liam shrugs. "Keeps things honest."

"Or slow," Marcus says, voice dropping as he leans closer. "You feel that?"

Liam does. The house is wrong. Not in the way of dust or rot, but in the sense of a thing emptied too quickly. There's a faint aftertaste of burnt toast, with a chemical, sticky edge. He follows the vector, stepping out of the foyer into a split-level living room that runs the length of the north wing.

Every window here is panoramic. Even at this hour, forest shadows stretch over the snowfields. Down below, a black line of trees forms the horizon, and somewhere behind all that, the sound of a helicopter engine cooling.

"You want to split, or stick together?" Marcus asks.

"Together," Liam says. Not shaking the feeling that if they don't, one of them won't come back.

They sweep the ground floor, methodical. Kitchen: empty. Guest bath: empty. Office: a laptop still open, its screen blank except for a slow, hypnotic scroll of code. Marcus glances at it, then shudders.

"Looks like someone left in a hurry," Liam says.

"Or didn't leave at all," Marcus says. He points to a stairwell, there's a distant flicker reflecting off far surfaces—lights strobe haphazardly, chaotic. Damage?

They follow. Each step downward is slow, deliberate. The stairs cantilever, floating above the void of the lower level. Halfway down, another sensor triggers a ring of blue-white lights, anticipating their descent.

At the landing, the air is cold, but heavy. There's a hum—a low, rhythmic thrumming, like the world's largest data center resonating beneath their feet.

"You catch that?" Liam whispers.

Marcus nods. "Server farm. Probably the thing running the house. Who else but Lord Alexander Mercer would have a full A.I. install, with all the trimmings?"

"Okay." Liam smirks. "I'll avoid pairing my phone, then."

Marcus grins, nerves peeking at the edges.

The corridor beyond is darker, walls lined with more LEDs, but here the art is different: not photographs, but grainy, blown-up micrographs of neurons, axons, clusters of cells locked in the moment of firing. The effect is claustrophobic.

They clear the hall, ending at a glass door.

Marcus approaches badge first, held like a shield. "Federal agents!" he repeats.

Nothing. Not even an echo.

He pushes the door. It glides open on a pneumatic seal. Inside: a small room, one wall mirrored, the other holding a row of lockers and hooks. Lights beat out white flashes from the adjacent room's window just beyond.

"This is getting weird," Marcus says.

Liam scans the ceiling, looking for cameras. None visible.

There's a second door, this one heavier. A sticker on it reads: "CLEAN ACCESS ONLY." An ID badge reader waits for input. Clearly, they're not getting through there without one. Instead, Liam approaches the window for a look.

Beyond inch think polycarbonate, he makes out a space reminiscent of an airlock. Against the flickering white walls, the splash of blood is unmistakable, a spray spreading out from below.

Marcus whispers, "Oh, screw me. What happened here?"

Liam follows the trail down to the body slumped beneath.

Male, late forties, built like a wrestler past his prime. Eyes wide open, hands locked around his own SIG Sauer, its suppressor still in his mouth. There is blood—lots of it—mostly against the wall behind.

Marcus leans his head against the glass. "What the hell, buddy?"

"His skin still has color, no signs of lividity. Stay on guard," Liam responds. "This just happened."

Marcus turns, hand clamped over his own hairline. "He ate his own gun. Why?"

Liam is about to answer when he spots the second body.

Female, mid-forties, features somewhat obscured by the angle of her fall. She's curled up, clutching at her abdomen. Blood pools beneath, a spreading lake of it.

"Gunshot number two," Liam says, pointing to the matted hole in her shirt. The lanyard around her neck—its badge is missing. Straightening himself, he scans what he can of the crime scene. "No sign of the shooter. Looks like there are bullet holes in the walls though."

Marcus rubs his chin. "Yeah. Pretty random though. Shoot out?"

"I don't see another—"

A voice interrupts, clear as day: "Detectives. Is everything to your satisfaction?" It's the house AI, piped in from a speaker hidden in the mesh seams.

Liam lets out a breath and glances at the ceiling. "Who am I speaking to?"

"I'm Vanta," the voice says, as smooth as a marketing video. "An aspect of my function is to maintain the residence. This includes climate, security, and, in rare cases, visitor mediation. Is there a concern?"

Marcus looks at the ceiling, then back to the glass and the carnage beyond. "Yeah, there's a concern. You got any cameras in that chamber?"

"There are sensors and point-of-presence monitors," Vanta replies, chipper as a game show host. "For safety and privacy, all recording is ephemeral, zeroed-out after seventy-two hours, as is policy."

"Who was the last to enter?" Liam asks.

The pause is a shade too long. "I'm afraid my range of answers is limited due to any potential legal ramifications," Vanta says. "I have contacted legal, as previously stated."

Marcus looks at Liam, then the bodies. "Ask it who fired the weapon."

Liam, deadpan: "Vanta, who fired the weapon?"

"Mr. Linnet discharged his firearm five times. Twice into the walls, once into the ceiling, once into Ms. Kovács, once into himself."

Marcus's face goes blank. "He shot her, then killed himself?"

"That is correct," says Vanta.

"But why?" Liam asks.

The house is silent, then: "Unclear. Mr. Linnet experienced a period of significant emotional instability prior to the event."

"Yeah, I bet he did," Marcus mutters. "Can you replay the security footage of what happened?"

"Security system for the server level was disrupted at 18:15:07," Vanta says. "No visual or audio is available after that time."

Liam makes a note. "Was anyone else present before 18:15?"

"Yes. Mrs. Evelyn Cross was here, with both Ms. Kovács and Mr. Linnet."

A cold goes through Liam, deeper than the room's chill.

"Was she harmed?" he asks.

A beat, as if the AI is weighing its words.

"Mrs. Cross did depart. I did not detect a notable injury. She used Ms. Kovács's ID badge to exit the server level."

The cold runs up Liam's spine. "Vanta, did Mrs. Cross discharge a weapon at either Linnet or Kovács?"

"Mrs. Cross was not armed."

Marcus whistles, low and ugly. "Wait. I don't get it." He taps on the window to the slumped male. "That one has a silencer. Linnet and Kovács bring her down here to do what? Kill her? Instead, she walks, and now they're both dead."

Liam says, "Vanta, can you determine why Mr. Linnet did not kill Mrs. Cross?"

The system seems to stall, then says: "I cannot. This is an anomaly. It is inconsistent with Mr. Linnet's previous record."

Marcus scans the room again, this time presenting genuine fear. "So she's out here. Alive and probably gunning for Mercer."

Liam holsters his weapon, but doesn't relax. "Vanta, where is Mr. Mercer?"

"Mr. Mercer is in the east wing, level two, hospital suite."

"Anyone else present?"

"Mrs. Evelyn Cross."

Marcus grabs Liam's shoulder, his shared concern obvious. "Holy shi—"

"And Detectives," Vanta interjects. "I can also confirm Ms. Celeste Mercer's life signs have just ended."

Chapter Thirty-Three

Window on Recognition

With Celeste's passing, the room's light dims further, no doubt under Vanta's predictive sense. Something more calming for its master. Evie's heartbeat thuds in the silence, echoing off the darkened walls like sonar. Mercer still curls around his daughter's body, lips moving in prayers that aren't meant to be heard.

It's a dirge, and for a minute she almost succumbs to the cold comfort of stillness. The Harbinger is quiet now, coiled in the center of her chest, nothing more than frost on her heart.

The air shifts.

There's a three-beat delay—first her, then Mercer, then the world—before Vanta speaks.

"Mrs. Cross," the AI says, in its infinite-patient tone, "federal authorities have arrived on the premises. They arrived by helicopter, and are in the building. Shall I lead them here?"

For a moment, Evie doesn't answer. The question doesn't even parse.

She glances at Mercer. He doesn't move. Too hollowed out—just a spent fuel rod, still glowing, but dead to everything but his own radioactive sorrow.

"No," she says, and is startled by the sound of her own voice, raw and wrong. "No, I... would not." She has no excuse for why. But what else can she say?

The system gives a half-second, maybe its only show of disappointment in this whole affair. "I can also recommend alternate exit strategies," Vanta offers, almost like a sommelier. "Would you prefer those?"

Evie steadies herself on an IV stand. Her hands are trembling, not from adrenaline—no, she's on the far side of that curve now. The shakes are what's left after a body spends its entire reserve in one go.

She moves to the window. Its opaque glass transitions to clear. Beyond the double panes and across the airfield is the blue and white chopper. Bone-white grounds span the distance between, then the mountain beyond.

Her body tenses, ready to bolt.

Evie scans the grounds for any sign of a SWAT perimeter, but there's just the single chopper. No cruisers. No dog teams. Whoever is coming has jumped the red tape; it's personal, or so classified that local law doesn't get a sniff. Advance team? Maybe it's just the Bureau and a local?

Or maybe it's because of her.

Mercer is not a threat anymore. He's not even the target. He's just a vessel, emptied of purpose.

Evie looks at him. "Guess you're going to have your chance to confess after all."

He rocks on his knees, hands tightening around the cooling hand of his daughter. "What would be the point?" he mutters. "I've already lost everything."

Evie's phone vibrates, a single pulse. She nearly laughs at the irrelevance—who in the world could possibly be texting her at this moment?—but then she glances down. It's a Virginia number. She doesn't recognize it, but the message is short.

SMS: RUN

No signature.

Evie's breath tightens. She presses her forehead to the glass, senses the world's sudden acceleration. Her old animal sense that's kept her alive when every job, every case, every horror demanded she find a way to the exit.

She pivots.

So enwrapped in his own grief, Mercer doesn't notice her depart.

Evie moves to a rear door. The glass is cold under her palm; the world outside is a theater of light and angles.

"Vanta," she says, "I'll need that way out after all."

The AI responds immediately. "There is a secondary stairwell two doors left, service only. Egress through the kitchen and then the patio. I can offline internal security for forty-five seconds. The Detectives are on their way up. CtrlZ says to hurry."

Oh!

She moves.

The door hisses open to a low, persistent hum of hidden servers, and the soft, desperate tick of her own boots replaces the house's endless hush. The corridor is empty. She passes through rooms full of art and dead electronics, with no signs of life anywhere. Not even a security detail. It's as if the whole mansion has surrendered.

Down the stairwell, past the climate-sealed kitchen, and out onto the side patio.

The cold is a physical slap. She almost drops.

"Seven seconds," Vanta says from a ground speaker. "You're about to be in view. Recommend concealment."

Evie darts across the flagstone, ducking under the bare claws of some designer shrub. She shimmies along the wall until she hits the east wing, the wall furred in ice, and scrambles along the maintenance path until the ground dips and gives her some cover.

She hears the chopper now, closer: the offbeat percussive that's always sounded to her like a war drum.

There is no jacket to keep Evie warm, only June's scarf. Her hands are raw, knuckles split from the cold, but she ignores it.

At the garden's edge, she turns to look back.

Up in the suite, the window is lit, and in it—framed as if within a panoramic photo—stands Liam Hayes. Though backlit, she'd know those strong shoulders anywhere.

He doesn't move. Just stands there, scanning down at the garden as if predicting her flight path from the jump.

She stands.

Her silhouette unfolds from the hedge. She holds her ground, hands bare, nothing threatening in her posture. Maybe that's why Liam stays still, watching her through the glass. A pause, then his hand lifts, presses flat to the thick pane, a single, unmistakable signal.

He's not here to chase her. Not really. He's here for her.

Evie nearly chokes on compulsion. She quashes it and instead waits for the few seconds it takes to afford her some good sense. Liam pivots, his features contort, resolve, then the lamp above him halos his head and she can see the exhaustion in the angle of his jaw.

The moment feels impossibly long. Her impulse is to go to him, to let the next few seconds ride on whatever might be. Maybe there's a world in which they could have made it work, become a team, found some new variable together.

But not this world.

She blinks the cold from her eyes, turns away from the mansion, and bolts for the driveway.

Behind her, the chopper's engine is spooling down, wind shunting the trees sideways. If it's just him she's got maybe sixty seconds before he can catch up to her.

Evie slams through the last rows of shrub, leaps a low wall, and sprints for her Ford Fiesta, still parked in the drive. For a second, she expects to see blue lights, an ambush. But it's empty, her keys still in the ignition.

She dives inside, slams the door, and for a moment is blinded by her own breath fogging the windshield.

Evie doesn't start the car immediately.

She sits, hands clutching the wheel, heart racing faster than the Ford's four-cylinder could ever manage. She glances up at the mansion, at the window where Hayes remains standing.

Maybe he's watching. Maybe he's waiting to see how far she goes.

"Go," she whispers, to herself, to June, to the thing that's held her together all these months.

The engine is barely up to the cold, but it turns over. She throws the car into gear. Gunning it, Evie fishtails on the icy road, and then she's tearing away from the compound, the mountains swallowing her up with every meter.

There's no going back.

Somewhere out in the white wilds, is a world that doesn't know her name. Maybe it's enough.

Maybe it isn't.

But for now, this variable is hers alone.

Chapter Thirty-Four

Masks of Intention

Marcus's eyes take a second to adjust to the dim hospital-like suite, much warmer than the rest of the house by a margin. The famous billionaire tycoon, Alexander Mercer, is on the floor. He slouches against a wall, his hands still clutching the edge of a bed like it might keep him from being swept away. Above, the medical monitors are all flat lines. Their readouts now only render a corpse in perfect linear detail.

For a span, Marcus just studies Mercer. He catalogues his every micro-expression: the slackness of the face, the reddening at the orbital rims, the pitch and timbre of his breathing. Suicidal? Doesn't seem immediate. There's a spent, simmering edge to the man's despair, but not the type to check out until he's made an audience of it.

Liam's boots are a whisper on the carpet behind. He turns away from the huge scenic window, thumb crooked into his belt, giving the place its due without pushing forward. To Marcus, this is the essence of law enforcement: two men, each pretending to be the least dangerous thing in the room.

He walks a slow perimeter of the suite, inventorying its elements. There's no sign of a struggle—no upended furniture, no misplaced tubes or toppled equipment. The body of Celeste Mercer lies perfectly still, features unblemished, hair lovingly arranged. Her left hand rests on her sternum, a gesture so staged it feels like a religious icon.

Marcus checks the med monitors, then flicks his gaze to Mercer, waiting for the man to notice him. When he doesn't, Marcus clears his throat. "Mr. Mercer. I'm a federal agent. I need you to answer a few questions. What's happened here?"

Mercer's fingers tighten around the mattress edge, whitening the nail beds.

Marcus exchanges glances with Liam, who gives the world's smallest nod: It's your job, profiler. Go for it.

He squats down, and flips open his badge.

"I understand there was a woman, Evelyn Cross, just here. She's a person-of-interest. Walk me through what happened," Marcus says, keeping his tone as neutral as possible. "From the time Mrs. Cross entered until... now."

Mercer's voice, when it comes, is unfiltered pain. "She accused me. Told me I had killed her daughter. Then she left." He sags, all the energy going out of him. "I didn't do it. I just... I just wanted to save my own daughter. Couldn't do that either."

Marcus's mind is already sprinting through half a dozen permutations. So, Evie didn't come to kill this Mercer? If so, and the body count on the server level is exactly as reported, then what the hell happened between those two? Was her revenge to kill his daughter? He glances at the IV, at the power source for the monitors.

Everything is still plugged in.

He's about to ask again, but Liam cuts in, voice softer. "Is there any medication present, Mr. Mercer, that she could have used to—?"

"No." Mercer shakes his head. "No one was poisoned. It was just her. She didn't even touch Celeste."

Marcus studies the man, the slight lateral flick that says he's remembering in detail. "You sure about that?"

Instead of answering the question, Mercer just tightens his death-gripped on the mattress, breathing through his teeth. The next sound comes from the wall, not the man.

"Mr. Mercer." Vanta takes on a less-pleasant register. "I have received a text response from your legal team. They have been advised of the current circumstances. You are strongly recommended to refrain from further comment until they are present."

Marcus, mid-inhale, lets the air out slow. Typical. Of course, the goddamn AI would lawyer his only suspect. It sticks in his craw, being bested by a glorified Alexa with tenure.

He picks up the nearest chair and pivots it so he's at Mercer's level, even as the man withers away in real time. "Great." Marcus glances back to Liam. "Wouldn't want you to incriminate yourself without your little Supreme Court on speed dial."

Mercer just sits, compacted into misery.

Marcus thumbs at a notepad app on his phone, scribbling lines in the ledger of what little Mercer has shared. He pats his own pant leg, thumping out thoughts of what next. How about directing elsewhere?

He looks up to the unseen voice. "Vanta, can you play back the last two minutes of life support telemetry and/or feeds for this room?"

The AI responds calmer than expected: "Of course, Agent Vaughn. Displaying now."

A split screen pops into being on the nearest wall. It shows the suite at 200 percent normal speed, the timeline clicking forward in the lower corner. Marcus watches Evie enter, sees the way she approaches the bed. Then, just as she retreats, Alexander becomes startled. He falls from his chair—wildly swats at the air while crawling backwards.

At timestamp minus one minute, the monitors on Celeste's bed jump, the oxygenation value spikes, and for a second, her eyes open.

Then the monitor's numbers begin to collapse. The blood oxygen drops in a neat, mechanical ramp. The heart rate stutters, pings zero, and her father lunges forward. His arms outstretched, desperate to reach the life support machines, yet...

There's a glitch in the video. Must be. Mr. Mercer's body seems suspended mid-leap in the gap between. Some freeze-frame glitch, for sure. But the time code continues to tick erroneously.

"Pause it." Marcus requests. "What just happened there?"

Vanta replies, "Mrs. Cross did not touch the patient, nor interact with the medical equipment. However, at 18:22:05, the ECMO machine was switched off and ceased operation."

Liam comes in alongside Marcus, furrowing his brow. "Switched off from where?"

"Direct from the machine terminal in this room," Vanta says.

Marcus side-eyes the unseen voice. "That can't be right. There's no one close enough to reach it, Vanta."

"Incorrect," Vanta chirped. "My data leads have been monitoring all aspects of the device since installation. A biometric response was recorded on the switch."

"Who's?" Marcus asks.

"Celeste Mercer's," Vanta says.

There is a silence so complete it practically achieves mass.

Liam murmurs, "Dead woman's hand."

Marcus glances at Mercer, whose face is now a smear of resentment. "Mr. Mercer, are we honestly saying your daughter... logged herself out?"

Mercer's mouth twists, but nothing comes out.

Marcus runs a hand over his jaw. "Vanta, did you see anything unusual—any other persons present, any other irregularities?"

The system pauses, as if thinking. "Negative, Agent Vaughn. I detected only those present and accounted for. No other signals, no other persons."

Liam looks at Marcus, and for a moment they are unified in a kind of awe: not of technology, but of the sheer, unaccountable weirdness that haunts the margins of their world.

"Huh. No way. This cannot be another suicide. That guy downstairs and now this?" Marcus spits out. Celeste appeared comatose in the video, functionally brain-dead. There's no way.

Vanta breaks the spell: "Mr. Mercer, your legal team has been notified of your daughter's passing. You have my sincerest condolences. I have a portfolio of respectable and established mortuary services. Shall I run their staff through screening protocols?"

Liam shakes his head. "Really on-the-spot, Vanta."

Marcus sighs. He crouches next to Mercer, giving the man space to grieve but not enough to bolt or grab something. "Mr. Mercer, I know this is the worst day of your life, but we're going to need you to come with us. You'll be protected, and you'll be given a chance to set the record straight."

Mercer stares at the floor, and nods.

Sliding back the chair, Marcus stands. He pulls out his phone, dials Haden on its secure channel.

The line clicks, and Haden's voice cuts like a surgical instrument: "Report."

"We have Mercer alive. Daughter, not so much. We also have a second crime scene with two additional vics. Situation… hella' unclear. Our suspect is in the wind, but there's evidence she was here moments before death."

Haden doesn't miss a beat. "Have you secured the bodies?"

"We'll lock things down," Marcus says. "Mercer is… compliant. No threat."

"Understood. My team is thirty out."

Liam, listening in, mouths 'thirty?' with a look of disbelief.

Marcus covers the receiver. "Feds… Always padding the numbers," he mutters.

Before he can say more, the line stutters—then another voice, colder, more harsh, rides in.

"Special Agent Vaughn, this is Beatrice Calder, SAC Washington Field. You will secure the scene, detain all involved, and stand by for my arrival. Is that clear?"

It's not a question.

Marcus flexes his jaw. "Perfectly."

Calder adds, "Agent Haden, we have reason to believe this residence is the locus for a national security event. Your agent and Detective Hayes are now attached to my office until further notice."

Liam, overhearing, suppresses an eye-roll.

"Copy that," Haden responds, his boss sounding like he's agreeing to a bus schedule, not a new chain of command.

Calder continues, "Do not permit the subject, Mercer, or anyone else to communicate externally, nor interact further with the in-house A.I. system. All personal electronics are to be surrendered. Is this understood?"

"Crystal," Marcus says.

"Sit tight," Calder says. "We'll be there in eighteen."

The line clicks off, as sudden and cold as the air outside.

Marcus pockets his phone and turns to Liam. "Well. Now I know how that feels."

Liam shrugs. "Welcome to the club."

Marcus regards Mercer, then at the panorama of snow outside, and finally at the lifeless, perfect corpse on the bed.

Somewhere out there, Evie is running free. Maybe. Just maybe he should delete that Virginia VIOP account he texted her from.

Chapter Thirty-Five

Now What?

Evie makes the first three switchbacks with the detached concentration of a person piloting a body that's not strictly her own. The Ford's windshield ripples with old stress lines, every rut in the icy slope magnified through the worn suspension.

Fresh snow is falling, and a skin of hard frost turns every hairpin into a physics problem. She guns the engine only at the straightaways, bracing for the tail end to fishtail and then bring it back with a pump of the brakes. Eyes on the ditches. On every third curve, she checks the rearview: nothing but the darkness, pin-pricked by the mansion's remaining exterior lights.

At the forest line, she forces herself to slow. She cuts north instead of the obvious descent back to town. If the Bureau or the local PD is setting up a net, she wants to be a glitch, not a prize fish.

The sound of her old engine is huge here, magnified by the forest, thumping in the hollow of her sternum. The Harbinger goes quiet, its presence receding into her gray matter, a prickle where it had been robust back there. She's not fooled; it's not done; this is only a remission.

Evie spends the next thirty minutes drafting random lefts and rights. Once, a pickup rattles past in the opposite direction—too slow for a cop, too erratic for a tail—but she still waits an extra two minutes before taking a more central avenue.

By the time she merges onto state route 191, the night descends fully at the edges. She resets her watch to Mountain Time, even though it's only a gesture. Time is the least of her problems.

On the other side of Jackson, she pulls into an off-bypass gas station, the sort with an all-night attached mini-mart and a parking lot bright enough to count the pores on your own face. She chooses a pump at the far end, facing the road.

Her Fiesta is running on fumes and dopamine. As the pump cycles through the gallons, she slouches back in the seat, letting her eyes focus on nothing for a long, raw minute.

Resting on the dash, Irina's access card glints with its perfect barcode and the microprint of a corporate logo. There is still a spot of dried blood on the edge—hers. The card is not large, not even as thick as a standard credit, but the weight it exerted on this universe is outsized. All thanks to its access to Vanta.

Evie turns it over, reading the name in full: KOVÁCS, IRINA. No title. Just the name, and a number.

She breathes in, lets it fill the hollow.

Evie recalls what Irina said:

> Not me. That task was outsourced, as so many things
> are. We had an exceptional operative, ideally suited to
> the task—one of my former assets from the Balkans.
> When the Cartographer case neared exposure, Mercer
> grew anxious. He asked me to have it intervened. Your
> family became not only leverage... but an example.

Evie's first instinct is to doubt it. She has mapped the world by trusting nothing, especially not last-minute villain monologues. But Irina's affect was never personal; she operated like a programming language, formality without malice. Lying at that point not only served no interest... it would have been rude. Irina prided herself too much. No, it made sense: someone was tasked, someone else pulled the trigger—international shell companies and subcontractors.

It should feel like a relief, but it does not.

If anything, the new vector is more dangerous. A professional killer with roots in the Balkans, a direct connection to Irina and—by extension—to whatever invisible system she folded into or out from.

The real problem is the former employer. Who the hell pays for a bespoke sociopath, then loses their best asset to a global database? Someone who was outbid, that's who.

She looks down at the card again. The last time she had evidence like this, she torched her career and her soul along with it. That last time, she let assertions get ahead of her. However, this time, there's nothing left to lose.

She powers up her laptop. It takes two minutes to get past the bootloader, another forty-five seconds to decrypt her Ethos channel.

At this hour, none of the old regulars should be green.

She checks again.

HeapMonk, RootMuse, and CtrlZ. All three show offline, but CtrlZ pings an auto-reply: On job. Pay up front or don't.

Well, there is that hundred grand she picked up at Greggs Cemetery. She's barely dipped into that to get here. Cash does have its benefits, just not so much online. How to get it to him? FedEx?? Not her concern. She can leave it to Z to work out.

> EVIE: CZ, you in?

The response is instantaneous. She doubts the person even uses a normal interface anymore—probably piped direct to their own cortex, or a black box at a data farm in Malta.

> CTRLZ: Oh, hey! Look who made it out!!

> EVIE: And away. A good bit away. But as a result, I'm on the run now. Might be a hot minute before I can catch up on the details.

Evie holds up the ID to her laptop cam and sends a photo to CtrlZ.

> EVIE: Need a scrub on this woman. Ex-Kaldria, now Mercer Global. Name's Irina Kovács. Got her badge. Want to know which spook house she actually worked for, and who was buying her talents previously. Can pay, but in cash only.

His next line comes in fast:

> CTRLZ: Saw your name just popped up on the ViCAP feed. You kill anyone?

She debates her answer.

> EVIE: It's not like that.

> EVIE: Not exactly.

> CtrlZ: Lol. Okay. Gimme 4 hours.

> EVIE: You're welcome to even more than that. I'll be off the grid till tomorrow. Let me know how we can make the exchange. You've guys have certainly earned it. Once we work out the details, I'll be bricking my laptop and phone.

Evie powers down and closes the lid. She lets the world compress into the circle of LED lights around the gas station.

Time to assess. Therefore, she needs to list. If the Bureau is tracking her, she can expect roadblocks at all points east, especially Cheyenne and Laramie. The Interstates will be a grid of state troopers and Feds, looking for a woman with a mixed-race profile and a car registered in Virginia. They'll know if she makes any ATM hits, uses a credit card. She needs to be less predictable.

Then there are the camera readers along the interstate. She should be able to bluff any cursory hits by swiping plates off a local vehicle. That'll be easier than rounding up a rental without revealing her identity. Once someone takes the time to delve in deeper, they'll figure out her course.

She thinks of the map. What's the least probable route?

North, through Montana. Cut across the old highways, then into Alberta by way of dirt roads. Her Spanish is passable; her French is merde. However, once she's across the Canadian border, her driver's license won't get flagged if she gets pulled over. She's certainly not about to flash her passport at a crossing station. Better to go around.

Evie leans back and lets herself fade for a few seconds. The gas station is empty except for a plow truck at the far edge, engine running while its driver hits the vending machine. The night is so bright it feels like a stage. She's never been more exposed.

Her hands are shaking, and not from the cold.

The refueling has been finished for nearly twenty minutes; the clerk probably assumes she's asleep at the wheel. She has had a window to rest, but not a large one.

She checks in the mirror again. No cars. Nothing.

The road ahead is a wound of black in the white fields. North, always north. A straight shot to Montana, then Canada, then obscurity. There really is no way back. The Bureau, or even Mercer's reach will catch up to her, eventually. But for a moment, there is a space between the variables. For a moment, she can pretend the future is a place she might someday see.

She glances at the access card one last time and slips it into her pocket. It's a puzzle piece, and she feels like the only person on Earth who knows what the picture is supposed to be.

Evie starts the engine. The world, for a second, comes alive.

She shifts into drive, and the Ford's tires catch the fresh salt laid over the blacktop. Evie will not look back. Not now, probably not ever.

Chapter Thirty-Six

The Veil Descends

Liam makes the rounds outside the Mercer estate, because it's what you do. Even when every single square foot has been swept and re-swept, there's something restorative in the walkabout, a ritual that makes air move. He loops the driveway twice, past the blue glow of the chopper and the Ford's frostbitten tire tracks. The main gate is a hundred yards out, black iron teeth biting at the edges of snow, and it's the last check on his list. It occurs to him, as he trudges up in the dark, that he's never seen a private residence with double-wired perimeter alarms, nor one that posts "Private Residence" in six languages.

Maybe this is part of why he does it: the sense that he sees how the other side of the world lives. Or maybe it's the anticipation, the near-certainty that something will go wrong if you stop believing it might.

At the crest of the drive, he stops and lets the air burn through his lungs. The mountains are hard to make out in the dark, but he knows they're there. He thinks of Evie, out in the somewhere. Hunted or running, most likely both.

The wind comes up hard, bending the trees along the road. Liam steps behind the gatepost and examines the latest state-of-the-art security system. Fairly minimal from outward glances. Bet there's a far piece more just behind it. He stands at rest, listening to the sound of his own heart.

Then the headlights appear.

Not one, not two—six, maybe seven sets of lights, all sync'd in a slow, almost balletic approach. No engine noise at first; just the punch and pulse of illumination as the vehicles thread the switchbacks. Black SUVs, identical right down to the ridged running boards, and the polarized windows. They drive in formation, half because of road conditions but also because that's the order they were given. Each one stops exactly two car-lengths behind the last.

Liam steps out onto the road, badge unclipped and ready, hands out and empty. The lead vehicle idles, engine nearly silent. The rest go dark, and for a moment there's just the ticking of metal and the wind moving through the pines.

The driver's window rolls down. There's a man behind the wheel who is all chin and jawline, eyes laser-straight ahead. There's no moment of sizing-up, no 'Can I help you?' or 'State your business.' Just a ten-count stare.

Liam waits for protocol, but there is none.

He steps to the window, holding his shield where it catches the dome light. "Detective Hayes, Missouri State. Who exactly are you folks with?"

The driver glances down, notes the badge, then back at Liam. "You're not only out of your jurisdiction, but you've already been given your SOP," he says. His voice is a Midwest drawl that's been run through a wood chipper. "So for now, you can wait here."

A door opens from the second SUV, and out steps a woman in a black windbreaker, hands tucked in the pockets. Her hair is a crisp iron-gray, cropped to the scalp. She wears pants with reinforced knees, boots that look standard-issue until you see the custom tread. There's no badge, no visible sidearm, but every inch of her says federal.

"Detective Hayes?" she calls. Her voice is clear and slicing. "Please come with me."

He checks the gate: it's been unlocked remotely, already swinging closed. Walking past the line of SUVs, Liam notes the passengers inside. None of them are talking, or even moving. Some wear suits, some wear polos over body armor, and all of them have the posture of people who haven't been surprised in a long time.

The woman waits until he's near, then waves him toward the side of the road, out of earshot. "Beatrice Calder. SAC, Washington Field," she says, low and clipped.

He overheard the name minutes before. No need to share his eavesdropping though. And Liam knows better than to ask questions. Not until he has a handle.

"SAC? Special Agent in Charge," he says, "Guessing you're Agent Haden's boss. Here for Mercer?"

She gives the smallest shake of her head. "Not him. The property." Her eyes flick past his shoulder, then back. "You and your Bureau friend will remain outside. No one re-enters the structure until my team has secured the data vault."

Liam wants to object. He even starts to, a hand half-lifting—but Calder steamrolls it with a smile that's all muscle, no warmth. She produces a phone, thumbs a speed dial, and angles it so he can hear the audio.

A familiar, exhausted voice—Haden's—comes on the line. "Detective Hayes, that scene is now under direct instruction from SAC Calder. I'd appreciate it if you stood by and complied with her team's directions. No need to ruffle any feathers. Our team is en route. We can rendezvous at the drive."

Calder ends the call, slides the phone away. "We'll set up an out-shelter with a heater and coffee. You'll wait there until further notice. Someone will bring you in when it's time."

Liam stares at her. "You're running this as a black site."

She shrugs, as if 'black site' is a compliment. "It's a national security incident. The less you know, the safer for everyone."

He wants to say "for whom," but it dies in his throat. Calder's already on to the next step. She motions to two of her men, who fall in behind her with perfect synchronization. They don't even glance at Liam as they pass.

The parade of agents files toward the house, a silent migration of efficient, heavy steps. Many carry black satchels. Two hauling outpost gear. No radios, no walkie traffic. At the mansion's threshold, a pair of them peel off, each producing a thin black keycard and tapping the lock in sequence. The door opens, swallowing the team in one seamless motion.

Liam stands in the wind, alone again.

He thinks of Marcus, still inside with Mercer, probably getting the same treatment—'Wait outside, touch nothing, don't talk to anyone.' He wonders what Evie would do in this moment. The answer is obvious: she'd already be in the basement, or halfway out of the country. Hell. She's probably already doing it.

Stepping into their erected tent, it's warm, surprisingly so, and rapidly assembled with tables, a generator, rations, bottled water, and laptops. A single massive thermos sits on a folding table, steaming faintly in the cold air. The chairs are collapsible. He sits, more out of spite than comfort.

Liam pours himself a coffee. It's bitter as bile, but he drinks it anyway. He waits.

Outside, the wind picks up, howling against the nylon walls. Under brilliant LEDs, the only thing to do is think, and Liam's brain is already tearing through possibilities. Who called this in, and why? Why does national security care about a dead billionaire and a pair of murdered fixers? What was so important in the server room that the FBI's own Behavioral Analysis Unit couldn't be trusted to see it?

He stares at the thermos, thinking of the chain of command, the comfort it used to give. Four years of military, a lifetime of procedure. You do your job; you trust the handoff, and maybe in the end, your tiny piece fits into the puzzle. But this—this is a new breed of case. No puzzle, just a void that eats other voids.

He drinks. He waits.

Time passes, or it doesn't. In the dead hours, it's hard to tell. At some point, the wind calms. The cold doesn't bite so much. He can almost hear the hum of the distant servers, out in the house, chewing up and spitting out the future.

He thinks about Evie: the way she saw patterns, the way she ignored every boundary and burned her own path here. He wonders what it would be like to just go, to let yourself become the variable instead of the sum.

When the tent flap finally opens, it's not another agent or a marshal. It's Marcus, pale and running on fumes.

"Yep. They're benching us," Marcus says. "It's not over. Not yet, at least."

Liam stands, rolling the tension from his shoulders.

He's ready.

Chapter Thirty-Seven

Spooks at the Door

An agent in a windbreaker and gloves signals for them to enter—Haden in the passenger seat, Webb behind the wheel, and Reyes riding along with their local PD in the SUV behind. After parking, Cass exits in time with Reyes as the first half of Haden's team catches up with the second. Marcus's face is a gravedigger's mask, all shadow under the brow, while Hayes walks with the exhaustion of a man who's been running a deficit for days.

The resort mansion is quite a different beast. Its entry vestibule is ringed with evidence cones, each one tagged with a barcode. More agents—maybe eighteen—fan through the lower level, some in Tyvek, others in Bureau navy. They move with the orchestration of a disaster drill.

Haden is met at the door by a tech he doesn't recognize, suit just tight enough to pinch at the elbows. The man doesn't offer a badge or a name, just says, "SAC Calder's waiting in the kitchen."

Following, he senses a minor escalation in the hush as they pass. With every five steps, a different instrument hums or vibrates. Every ten, an agent looks up, checks him off an invisible list, then erases from memory.

Mercer's kitchen is a retro-future workstation. Its center island is a slab of stone the color of a storm cloud, with a built-in induction burner and a half-dozen stools. Calder is by the far window, hands at her back, neck rigid as a dowel. She does not turn until the door shuts.

"Thomas," she says, like it's a performance review.

He feels the years contract and vanish. "Beatrice. Didn't expect to see you this far from D.C."

She's in her element. The kitchen, the scene, even the posture; it's all orchestration. She gives a small, precise smile. "I go where the case demands. In this instance, the case has outpaced Bureau protocols. I trust you tried to look up the brief."

Haden gestures at the windows, at the blur of motion in the halls. "No point. Seems the situation is well in hand."

"In hand, yes." Calder's eyes flick to the others. "You four. Haden will be with you in a moment. For now, you can linger in the dining room. Thomas, have a seat. We'll make this brisk."

While he sits on a stool, his team ambles back out of the room, closing the door behind them.

She circles a half-turn, then leans in just enough to fill the peripheral. "You've been point on this since the D.C. escalation. Even after Quantico cut your funding, you held the wheel. That's rare these days." She pauses, then softens the edge. "Rare, but appreciated."

He says nothing, waiting for the knife.

Calder glances at her own hands, then up. "The NSA is taking full jurisdiction on the server and digital asset end. We'll handle the perimeter, the local press, the bodies. What remains for the Bureau is strictly evidentiary. Mercer will never see a public court, let alone a trial. He's going away now."

Haden looks down at the island, not quite focusing. "Not exactly by-the-book, are we?"

"There can't be a book for this," she says, and for a blink she's almost likeable again.

She leans in, lowering her voice. "His Vanta system is the highest priority, not Mercer, not the fixers, not even the local law. The only reason your team is still here is that you have the best chance of explaining how any of this came to be. That way we can mitigate complications. I need your full assessment, unvarnished. Starting with how your investigation led to this place."

She straightens, hands back at parade rest, and continues, "Start with the Jackson Hole angle, here. The why."

He sits, weighing how to begin. There's a trembling in Haden's left hand, the knuckles twitching. He closes the fist. "It honestly started with the Cartographer returning to D.C. Our investigation got—"

She raises a finger. "I know what happened to your investigation. What's this have to do with Mercer? I need a motive. I need the thread."

Thomas nods, then clears his throat. "The first time I saw Evie Cross, I thought she was another Quantico algorithm. Just meat in the machine. She presented a data model that connected serial killings with the Bay Area suicides, and she did it in half the time my own team could have established a chain of custody. But—" he sips at the words, cautious, "—she was bright and driven. Even then. There was something about her that made every lead fresh and unexpected."

Calder's lips flatten, but she doesn't interrupt.

He goes on. "She was rocketing into becoming a career star. But then her daughter vanished, and she fell apart. Or that was the official narrative. My guess, she didn't fall apart at all. She got sharper. Evie just lost faith that anyone would be able to relate."

Calder's eyes lose the kill. "And you?"

"I mentored," Haden says, and it sounds damning even as he says it. "Others wanted to see if she was salvageable. If she could be," he hates the word, "—redirected."

Beatrice nods, almost with a pang. "Not your idea."

"No." Haden's hands drum the stone, small taps. "But it was my call to let her run with the resurfaced Cartographer case. I expected she might go rogue. Thought I could handle it."

There's a pause, thin and hostile. Calder breaks it. "But you didn't."

Haden laughs, just barely. "No. She's made a career out of not being handled."

Walking a circle around the island, Calder's voice is a whisper. "Why didn't you burn her out when you had the chance? You could have tagged her after the Cartographer snafu—"

He stops her there. "You don't burn out a mind like that. You let it run hot and see what else catches. And occasionally, it finds a way through the heat. I had faith she'd come through it."

"And this is that?" Calder asks.

"Can't say," he counters. "But then you don't want my philosophy. You want the timeline."

"Correct," Calder says. "But I also wanted to understand your loyalty."

He shakes his head. "My protégé didn't want loyalty. Evie wanted a world that made sense."

Calder allows herself a shadow of a smile. "Don't we all."

Outside the kitchen, an agent wheels by a cart loaded with hard drives, each one stickered and logged. The hum of cooling fans grows louder as the cart passes.

Calder glances at it, then turns back. "You'll be required to provide a written brief before you leave. For now, walk me through the last seventy-two hours. Make it clear."

He begins, his mind already lining the words up like dominoes.

"ViCAP flagged Evelyn Cross after the Kansas City Airport incident. She made herself visible—deliberately—by triggering pings in every database that tracked her. She wanted to be followed, which means she wanted an audience, not a cover. Cass here picked up the trail because she recognized the pattern, and Marcus was smart enough to trust that instinct. The others—Reyes, Hayes—were on the tail because they believed in supporting the team."

Calder's eyebrow twitches. "You don't believe she's dead?"

He considers, then shakes his head. "She's not. She's vanished, yes, but she's not gone. There's always another variable with her."

Calder doesn't correct him. "What about the... incident in the server room?"

He exhales. "You got me. I read your team's report. There's no logical explanation for what happened to Irina and her bodyguard. Only the aftermath."

Calder says, "We've no video. Not down there. That report is going off of purely classic forensics. Still, there has to be something more left out."

"Agreed. It's her," Haden says. "It's probably her. Evie must have found some anomaly in a system Ms. Kovács didn't pick up on until it was too late. That seems to be working out for my rogue agent pretty well."

Calder tilts her head as if trying to see if he's lost his mind. "Are you implying—"

He cuts in, voice cold. "I'm not implying anything. I'm saying you can follow the variables, or you can try to solve for x. But in the end, Evie... is... x."

Calder stands silent, perhaps for the first time since he's known her. She presses both hands flat on the stone, then leans down, nose almost to his.

"I respect your loyalty, Thomas. But from this moment, she is a nonentity. If she surfaces again, it will not be the Bureau that comes for her."

He nods, not trusting himself to answer.

Calder straightens, checks her phone, then says, "Get your team, debrief in the vestibule. I'll have a car waiting in thirty. Leave everything behind."

He stands, but as he does, she says, "And Thomas?"

He looks back.

"I need your written assessment by 8AM. Not just the facts. Your conclusion. All of it."

He nods, and this time the tremor in his hand is gone.

Haden leaves the kitchen, walks the corridor, and sees his team arrayed by the dining hall—Marcus pacing, Hayes standing with the slouch of a man who's realized his job is over, Webb and Reyes pressed together, whispering in each other's ears. None of them look at him, but he knows they're waiting.

He steps outside, breathes the mountain air, tastes the snow coming on the wind. He thinks of Evie, somewhere out there, a shadow in her own story.

The world is colder now.

He opens the shelter flap, and they all file in, silent, waiting for the last word.

He sits, the four of them ringed around him, and he says, "I'll make this short."

Marcus smirks.

Haden lets the seconds build, then says, "They're closing us out. From here, it's above our grade. Calder wants our statements, then we're done."

Hayes nods, no protest.

Reyes glances at Webb, who just breathes out, relieved.

He looks at them, each one. He thinks of all the times he's delivered this speech, the end of a case, the handoff to higher powers. It never gets easier.

"You are to leave all your things," he says. "Thirty minutes and we're out."

They nod, but Marcus holds back, eyes narrowed.

Haden glances from face to face, searching for some parting argument, some last gasp of protest. Nothing. He holds up a hand, flicks his fingers: Get to it. Not a command, but a release. The others break formation, dispersing to the sprawl of shelter benches and side tables. Marcus flips open a steno pad and begins writing immediately, a faint hiss of graphite. Webb, meticulous, cracks open her notebook and starts logging timestamps, cross-referencing them aloud in a murmur only Reyes can hear. Hayes, ever the minimalist, writes nothing at all.

Haden waits long enough to ensure most are well underway. Only then does he make space for his own frustrations. The world in here is still too close, too full of the unmourned. He buttons his jacket, tugging it tight at the throat, and heads out the tent flap.

The wind is up again, a fine haze of spindrift blurring the boundary between sky and ground. Haden stands in the lee where the incoming snow rips lateral lines over the grass. The world tastes unsalted, blank.

He doesn't even get two minutes.

Marcus steps out. "You think she's out there?"

Haden looks at the snow. "I know she is."

Marcus shakes his head. "Never believed in ghosts."

"You don't have to, Marcus. But, tell me," Haden says. "What exactly is left of a person when you've taken everything else of meaning away... if not that?"

Marcus shrugs. "Think it'll come to a good end?"

"No." Haden shakes his head. "Not yet."

He stands, tightening his coat. The world feels emptier, but also strangely possible.

Haden walks out to the drive, the cold burning his lungs. Ah, that first day he met Evelyn Cross—the sharpness of her voice, the brilliance in her eyes, the way she made everything else seem slow and imprecise.

If there's still a next time to be had, he won't waste it.

For now, there's a report to write...

...and a truth to bury.

Chapter Thirty-Eight

Just Watch

E vie runs north, half because she thinks it's safe, but also because of fewer variables in such empty spaces.

She plows ahead for hours. Clear blacktop runs out after Dubois; the rest is spindrift and raw surface, a slipstream of mindless motion. She stops for gas, but doesn't enter the store. Instead, she keeps her head down, gloves on, cash paid through the bulletproof partition. Her Ford's heater fights a losing battle; every exhale frosts the rearview mirror.

There's a moment, somewhere past 3AM, where she plans to depart from the path she's on. Don't take the straightaway. The time you lose in not going direct is time not being caught up to. She pulls off, engine idling, and begins her protocol.

First, the phone. Already off, she flips it, and with a small screwdriver from her kit, she cracks the shell. The battery comes out, then the SIM, both dropped into the glove box. She runs her thumb along the circuit board, half-expecting it to burn her. She's seen enough devices go sideways in the last year never to trust default settings.

Second, the laptop. She kills the Wi-Fi, then the Bluetooth, then everything but the barest kernel. The camera gets taped, then the mic—an old habit, but the only one worth having. She runs her hand along the bottom, checking for the thermal shadow of a powered tracker. Nothing.

Sitting for a moment, Evie breathes into her daughter's scarf, eyes tracing the horizon.

Then, with a turn of the wheel, she drives off, only northwest now.

Her motel selection is by mental algorithm: not the closest, not the cheapest, not the kind with Wi-Fi passwords taped to every surface. This one is mom-and-pop; its vacancy sign is a dull red pulse against the night. The lobby is empty except for an old TV muttering cable news.

The woman behind the counter has a face like a warning. "You just need the one night?" she asks, her words braided with the twang of back roads.

Evie nods, hands over the bills. "Do you have anything on the back side, away from the road?"

The woman gives her a look, but doesn't ask. She hands over a key—not a card, but a real, metal key, heavy in Evie's palm.

"Room Four. If you want heat, turn it up slow. Takes a while to catch."

Evie thanks her, then pauses, checking the windows, the sightlines, the angles to the parking lot. She's not expecting a tail, but she's new to this whole being on the run thing.

The room itself is smaller than most cells she's visited. The bedspread is older than her career. Its heater rattles in the corner like an old man with the shakes. She slides her bag onto the desk, sets up the laptop, and sits cross-legged on the bed.

Now for the ritual.

Evie knows she should wait until the next day. But technically, this early in the morning is just that. And she just needs to know if CtrlZ had any luck yet.

VPN, then Tor. She routes through three, no, five nodes, each in a country with more problems than she can count. She cracks her Ethos shell, triple-checks for anomalies in the handshake. It's clean—maybe cleaner than she expected. She runs the diagnostics anyway.

Only then does she let her pulse slow.

Her message queue alerts.

HeapMonk has left nothing but a bounce. RootMuse, silence. CtrlZ, the last thread already cold. But there is a new message, subject line blank. No sender, only a string of numbers and letters she's never seen before.

She pauses, hovering over the file.

This is how they get you.

The Harbinger is quiet, but then tech isn't really its thing.

She scans the attachment in a sandbox. If there's anything jinky inside, it'll get flagged and bombed out of virtual reality. Yet, once the sim runs itself... There's nothing—no payload, no exploit, just a compressed .jpg and a short text in the body.

She opens the message.

It reads:

> I've been informed you are sowing disharmony among my Maestros. I will have no more of that. You have not learned your lesson. There is more you can still lose.

Just watch.

Evie's mouth goes dry. The language—the phrase 'sowing dishar-mony among my Maestros'—sparks muscle-memory in her jaw. That was never disclosed. Only the originator would frame it with such arcane self-seriousness.

Her hands shake as she backtracks the meta-headers, looking for anything raw: geoloc, a fingerprint in the digital dust. Standard cloaking—but not total. In the bounce from Luxembourg to Kuala Lumpur, there's a bleed-over, a fraction of an IP block she recognizes from a mid-pandemic briefing at Quantico. It's not just a threat. It's proof.

She clicks the image.

It's a photo of a manila envelope splayed on a steel table—not a home or an office. No external marking. No codes, no glitter-paint, no return address . It's just a manila envelope. The kind that turns up under doors. In mail slots. Tucked under wipers.

Exactly the kind that appeared at her Virginia townhouse.

The one with June's braid.

Evie's breath hooks in her throat, a fish snagged on a barb. She clicks to full-screen. The JPEG is not high-resolution—she can see individual compression artifacts, the JPEG fractals. She checks the EXIF; it's been scrubbed, but the pixel noise says a low-light phone shot, possibly a burner.

She stares at the envelope for a long time.

This is not just a warning. It's someone telegraphing a consequence. It's coming.

'Just watch.'

The Harbinger stirs, deep in her hippocampus. There is a desire to respond, to fight back, but how?

From somewhere primordial—deep under the cortex—something short-circuits. Evie stares at the screen, at that JPEG, and the trace elements of anger in her blood catch fire. The Harbinger flexes inside her skull, more presence than voice, and this time it is Evie who unleashes.

She grinds the heel of her palm into the laptop's hinge, popping it off the desk onto the carpet. It lands with a hollow thunk. She kneels, digs her thumb into the power button, holding it as if choking out a windpipe. The whir of the fan dies.

Her breath sits at the threshold of a scream, but she bites it back. Instead, she grabs the base, slams the edge down—once, twice, three times—until the screen fractures and splits into black veins. She hits it again, then a few more times for the sheer, irrational pleasure of the violence. The glass splits, shedding corners that scatter like sugar on the synthetic blue carpet.

Evie sits back, panting. There is a static charge on her arms, inside her molars. She leans forward, forehead pressed to the laptop's cold chassis, and waits for the compulsion to fade.

It doesn't.

She reaches into her bag, finding the Glock—cold and hard. Its polymer grip is rough under her skin. She goes through the motions: drops the mag, racks the slide, clears the chamber. Satisfied, she turns the gun around and brings the butt down on the laptop's hard drive, over and over, a raw hammer bounded by the spring and impact in her bones.

Eventually, the drive's faceplate is a crumpled, gray wound. She keeps going until the gun's magazine well bites into her palm and leaves a crescent-shaped bruise. Only then does something physical—something outside of all thought—cut through the frenzy. Her hands tremble. The room smells of hot plastic and her own sweat.

Her world returns in increments. That vibrating heater. The lens of condensation on the single-paned window. The way her knuckles are bleeding, each drop instantly stipples onto the carpet with red.

She sits. Breathes. Stares at her hands.

A sound unspools from her lips, almost a laugh, almost a sob.

In the glass of the blackened laptop screen, she sees her own face—fractured by the damage, multiplied by the shards.

Behind her, or maybe inside, the Harbinger settles. Its calm touch sooths across her shoulders.

Evie bundles the laptop in a towel, shoving the gun back in her waistband. She wraps the stark mess in a towel, using the ragged edge to mop the blood from her hands. The pain is sharp but useful, a focused blade scraping her nerves back into control.

She glances at the battered shell of the laptop, then out the window.

There is nothing but her own Ford, iced to the doors, and a battered pickup with a Montana plate. No headlights. No movement.

She waits. Ten seconds, twenty.

'Just watch.'

She closes the curtain, then stands by the door, her breath slowing.

If they want her, she'd be happy to go to them. But this isn't that. No. They want her to suffer. Evie almost cannot allow herself to consider it, but...

Last time it was her daughter.

She glances down at the scarf—June's scarf—and wonders what else she can lose?

Everything.

Spectral Hunter: Winter's Maw

Evelyn Cross is a ghost of her former self, and the Canadian North is the perfect place to vanish.

A former FBI profiler, Evie is on the run, trading her old life for the icy anonymity of the Saskatchewan. She only wants to hide—but the small town of La Ronge is already at a breaking point. When a local hunter goes missing, Evie is drawn into a desperate search.

But in this cold and vast silence, not all monsters are myth.

When Evie's profiler instincts clash with legends of the Wendigo—a spirit of insatiable hunger—she discovers the true predator may be bound where she least expects.

Cornered and exposed, Evie must face a terrifying choice. Unleash the thing threatening to consume her—the Harbinger—or turn a blind eye to a hunting killer. To save the innocent is to risk what vestiges of humanity she has.

Prepare for a bone-chilling journey through vengeance, morality, and the blurred boundaries between humanity and monstrosity in WINTER'S MAW—a FREE, heart-stopping paranormal short story set between Books 3 and 4 of the Spectral Hunter Series. Click through to read the story. Plus, with your email, you'll get notified when new books release. **No spam—*just the chills you crave.***

FREE Short Story / No Spam

Submit a Review

If **This Vanta Mirror** resonated with you, a short review on Amazon would mean the world to me. It helps other readers discover the story and supports my work. Share what you loved most (a favorite scene, character, or moment that stayed with you) and whether you'd recommend it; even a sentence or two makes a huge difference.

Thank you for taking a moment to leave your thoughts—your voice helps this book find its next reader.

Also from ALVS

The Books of Ruein
Death has its own kind of grace.

When the gods stopped listening, Ruein learned to whisper to the dead.

Once a mother, wife, and reluctant necromancer, she has clawed her way through curses, godless realms, and divine betrayals to protect the one thing that still matters—her family. But every spell cast in love carries a shadow, and Ruein's has begun to stir.

From the smoke of Vandraport's streets to the frozen citadels of Haraden, Ruein is hunted by powers both mortal and celestial. To save her son, she'll forge impossible alliances: with dragons, killers, and even the Lightbringer sworn to destroy her. Yet the deeper she delves into the underworld of magic, the more she risks becoming what she most fears.

Because the dead are never done with you.

Wickedly funny, brutal, and unflinchingly human, The Books of Ruein is a dark fantasy saga of necromancy, faith, and the cost of love in a world that eats its own gods.

For readers of The Witcher, The First Law, and The Sandman, who prefer their fantasy rich with blood, ash, and gallows humor.

Now Available on Amazon

UFO Science
Unraveling the Phenomena

Step beyond speculation and into discovery. The UFO Science Series takes you on an unprecedented exploration of the evidence, physics, and mysteries shaping humanity's understanding of Unidentified Anomalous Phenomena and the enigmatic patterns that appear in our fields.

In Book One, uncover the revolutionary science that may drive advanced UAP craft. From declassified Pentagon encounters to breakthrough theories by pioneers like T. Townsend Brown and Jack Sarfatti, you'll gain a clear and comprehensive view of the physics that could be redefining reality itself.

In Book Two, delve into the geometric and biological mysteries of crop circles—where intricate designs meet scientific data. Explore soil anomalies, eyewitness accounts, and the unexplained precision behind these vast formations that continue to defy conventional reasoning.

Blending research, case studies, and cutting-edge hypotheses, this series challenges readers to look closer, think deeper, and question what they thought they knew about the world around them.

The frontier of discovery is here.

Are you ready to see what's been hiding in plain sight?

Now Available on Amazon